SUMMER SUMMER
MORNING, NIGHT

SUMMER SUMMER MORNING, NIGHT

Ray Bradbury

Edited by
DONN ALBRIGHT, *Pratt Institute*
and
JON ELLER, *Indiana University*

SUBTERRANEAN PRESS • 2008

First U.S. Edition

ISBN 978-1-59606-202-3

Subterranean Press
PO Box 190106
Burton, MI 48519

www.subterraneanpress.com

CONTENTS

A Note on the Texts

The text for "End of Summer" is based on the version collected by Bradbury in Driving Blind (1997). The texts of all other previously published stories in this collection are based on the earliest published versions. I am grateful to David Spiech, my colleague at Indiana University's Institute for American Thought, for copy editing this volume.

To Jon Eller with love.

Ray

END OF SUMMER

ONE. TWO. HATTIE'S lips counted the long, slow strokes of the high town clock as she lay quietly on her bed. The streets were asleep under the courthouse clock, which seemed like a white moon rising, round and full, the light from it freezing all of the town in late summer time. Her heart raced.

She rose swiftly to look down on the empty avenues, the dark and silent lawns. Below, the porch swing creaked ever so little in the wind.

She saw the long, dark rush of her hair in the mirror as she unknotted the tight schoolteacher's bun and let it fall loose to her shoulders. Wouldn't her pupils be surprised, she thought; so long, so black, so glossy. Not too bad for a woman of thirty-five. From the closet, her hands trembling, she dug out hidden parcels. Lipstick, rouge, eyebrow pencil, nail polish. A pale blue negligee, like a breath of vapor. Pulling off her cotton nightgown, she stepped on it, hard, even while she drew the negligee over her head.

She touched her ears with perfume, used the lipstick on her nervous mouth, penciled her eyebrows, and hurriedly painted her nails.

She was ready.

She let herself out into the hall of the sleeping house. She glanced fearfully at three white doors. If they sprang open now, then what? She balanced between the walls, waiting.

The doors stayed shut.

She stuck her tongue out at one door, then at the other two.

She drifted down the noiseless stairs onto the moonlit porch and then into the quiet street.

The smell of a September night was everywhere. Underfoot, the concrete breathed warmth up along her thin white legs.

"I've always wanted to do this." She plucked a blood rose for her black hair and stood a moment smiling at the shaded windows of her house. "You don't know what I'm doing," she whispered. She swirled her negligee.

Down the aisle of trees, past glowing street lamps, her bare feet were soundless. She saw every bush and fence and wondered, "Why didn't I think of this a long time ago?" She paused in the wet grass just to feel how it was, cool and prickly.

The patrolman, Mr. Waltzer, was wandering down Glen Bay Street, singing in a low, sad tenor. As he passed, Hattie circled a tree and stood staring at his broad back as he walked on, still singing.

When she reached the courthouse, the only noise was the sound of her bare toes on the rusty fire escape. At the top of the flight, on a ledge under the shining silver clock face, she held out her hands.

There lay the sleeping town!

A thousand roofs glittered with snow that had fallen from the moon.

She shook her fists and made faces at the town. She flicked her negligee skirt contemptuously at the far houses. She danced and laughed silently, then stopped to snap her fingers in all four directions.

A minute later, eyes bright, she was racing on the soft lawns of the town.

She came to the house of whispers.

She paused by a certain window and heard a man's voice and a woman's voice in the secret room.

Hattie leaned against the house and listened to whispering, whispering. It was like hearing two tiny moths fluttering gently inside on the window screen. There was a soft, remote laughter.

Hattie put her hand to the screen above, her face the face of one at a shrine. Perspiration shone on her lips.

"What was that?" cried a voice inside.

Like mist, Hattie whirled and vanished.

When she stopped running she was by another house window.

A man stood in the brightly lighted bathroom, perhaps the only lighted room in the town, shaving carefully around his yawning mouth. He had black hair and blue eyes and was twenty-seven years old and every morning carried to his job in the railyards a lunch bucket packed with ham sandwiches. He wiped his face with a towel and the light went out.

Hattie waited behind the great oak in the yard, all film, all spiderweb. She heard the front door click, his footsteps down the walk, the clank of his lunch pail. From the odors of tobacco and fresh soap, she knew, without looking, that he was passing.

Whistling between his teeth, he walked down the street toward the ravine. She followed from tree to tree, a white veil behind an elm, a moon shadow behind an oak. Once, he whirled about. Just in time she hid from sight. She waited, heart pounding. Silence. Then, his footsteps walking on.

He was whistling the song "June Night."

The high arc light on the edge of the ravine cast his shadow directly beneath him. She was not two yards away, behind an ancient chestnut tree.

He stopped but did not turn. He sniffed the air.

The night wind blew her perfume over the ravine, as she had planned it.

She did not move. It was not her turn to act now. She simply stood pressing against the tree, exhausted with the shaking of her heart.

It seemed an hour before he moved. She could hear the dew breaking gently under the pressure of his shoes. The warm odor of tobacco and fresh soap came nearer.

He touched one of her wrists. She did not open her eyes. He did not speak.

Somewhere, the courthouse clock sounded the time as three in the morning.

His mouth fitted over hers very gently and easily.

Then his mouth was at her ear and she was held to the tree by him. He whispered. So *she* was the one who'd looked in his windows the last three nights! He kissed her neck. She, *she* had followed him, unseen, last night! He stared at her. The shadows of the trees fell soft and numerous all about, on her lips, on her cheeks, on her brow, and only her eyes were visible, gleaming and alive. She was lovely, did she know that? He had thought he was being haunted. His laughter was no more than a faint whisper in his mouth. He looked at her and made a move of his hand to his pocket. He drew forth a match, to strike, to hold by her face, to see, but she took his hand and held it and the unlit match. After a moment, he let the matchstick drop into the wet grass. "It doesn't matter," he said.

She did not look up at him. Silently he took her arm and began to walk.

Looking at her pale feet, she went with him to the edge of the cool ravine and down to the silent flow of the stream, to the moss banks and the willows.

He hesitated. She almost looked up to see if he was still there. They had come into the light, and she kept her head turned away so that he saw only the blowing darkness of her hair and the whiteness of her arms.

He said, "You don't have to come any further, you know. Which house did you come from? You can run back to wherever it is. But if you run, don't ever come back; I won't want to see you again. I couldn't take any more of this, night after night. Now's your chance. Run, if you want!"

Summer night breathed off her, warm and quiet.

Her answer was to lift her hand to him.

NEXT MORNING, as Hattie walked downstairs, she found Grandma, Aunt Maude, and Cousin Jacob with cold cereal in their tight mouths, not liking it when Hattie pulled up her chair. Hattie wore a grim, highnecked dress, with a long skirt. Her hair was a knotted, hard bun behind her ears, her face was scrubbed pale, lean of color in the cheeks and lips. Her painted eyebrows and eyelashes were gone. Her fingernails were plain.

"You're late, Hattie," they all said, as if an agreement had been made to say it when she sat down.

"I know." She did not move in her chair.

"Better not eat much," said Aunt Maude. "It's eight-thirty. You should've been at school. What'll the superintendent say? Fine example for a teacher to set her pupils."

The three stared at her.

Hattie was smiling.

"You haven't been late in twelve years, Hattie," said Aunt Maude.

Hattie did not move, but continued smiling.

"You'd better go," they said.

Hattie walked to the hall to take down her green umbrella and pinned on her ribboned flat straw hat. They watched her. She opened the front door and looked back at them for a long moment, as if about to speak, her cheeks flushed. They leaned toward her. She smiled and ran out, slamming the door.

THE GREAT FIRE

THE MORNING THE great fire started, nobody in the house could put it out. It was mother's niece, Marianne, living with us while her parents were in Europe, who was all aflame. So nobody could smash the little window in the red box at the corner and pull the trigger to bring the gushing hoses and the hatted firemen. Blazing like so much ignited cellophane, Marianne came downstairs, plumped herself with a loud cry or moan at the breakfast table and refused to eat enough to fill a tooth cavity.

Mother and father moved away, the warmth in the room being excessive.

"Good morning, Marianne."

"What?" Marianne looked beyond people and spoke vaguely. "Oh, good morning."

"Did you sleep well last night, Marianne?"

But they knew she hadn't slept. Mother gave Marianne a glass of water to drink and everyone wondered if it would evaporate in her hand. Grandma, from her table chair, surveyed Marianne's fevered eyes. "You're sick, but it's no microbe," she said. "They couldn't find it under a microscope."

"What?" said Marianne.

"Love is godmother to stupidity," said father, detachedly.

"She'll be all right," mother said to father. "Girls only seem stupid because when they're in love they can't hear."

"It affects the semicircular canals," said father. "Making many girls fall right into a fellow's arms. I *know*. I was almost crushed to death once by a falling woman and let me tell you—"

"Hush." Mother frowned, looking at Marianne.

"She can't hear what we're saying; she's cataleptic right now."

"He's coming to pick her up this morning," whispered mother to father, as if Marianne wasn't even in the room. "They're going riding in his jalopy."

Father patted his mouth with a napkin. "Was our daughter like this, Mama?" he wanted to know. "She's been married and gone so long, I've forgotten. I don't recall she was so foolish. One would never know a girl had an ounce of sense at a time like this. That's what fools a man. He says, Oh what a lovely brainless girl, she loves me, I think I'll marry her. He marries her and wakes up one morning and all the dreaminess is gone out of her and her intellect has returned, unpacked, and is hanging up undies all about the house. The man begins running into ropes and lines. He finds himself on a little desert isle, a little living room alone in the midst of a universe, with a honeycomb that has turned into a bear trap, with a butterfly metamorphosed into a wasp. He then immediately takes up a hobby: stamp collecting, lodge-meetings or—"

"How you *do* run on," cried mother. "Marianne, tell us about this young man. What was his name again? Was it Isak Van Pelt?"

"What? Oh—Isak, yes." Marianne had been roving about her bed all night, sometimes flipping poetry books and reading incredible lines, sometimes lying flat on her back, sometimes on her tummy looking out at dreaming moonlit country. The smell of jasmine had touched the room all night and the excessive warmth of early spring (the thermometer read 55 degrees) had kept her awake. She looked like a dying moth, if anyone had peeked through the keyhole.

This morning she had clapped her hands over her head in the mirror and come to breakfast, remembering just in time to put on a dress.

Grandma laughed quietly all during breakfast. Finally she said "You must eat, child, you *must*." So Marianne played with her toast and got half a piece down. Just then there was a loud honk outside. That was Isak! In his jalopy!

"Whoop!" cried Marianne and ran upstairs quickly.

The young Isak Van Pelt was brought in and introduced around.

When Marianne was finally gone, father sat down, wiping his forehead. "I don't know. This is too much."

"You were the one who suggested she start going out," said mother.

"And I'm sorry I suggested it," he said. "But she's been visiting us for six months now, and six more months to go. I thought if she met some nice young man—"

"And they were married," husked grandma darkly, "why, Marianne might move out almost immediately—is *that* it?"

"Well," said father.

"Well," said grandma.

"But now it's worse than before," said father. "She floats around singing with her eyes shut, playing those infernal love records and talking to herself. A man can stand so much. She's getting so she laughs all the time, too. Do eighteen-year-old girls often wind up in the booby hatch?"

"He seems a nice young man," said mother.

"Yes, we can always pray for that," said father, taking out a little shot glass. "Here's to an early marriage."

The second morning Marianne was out of the house like a fireball when first she heard the jalopy horn. There was not time for the young man even to come to the door. Only grandma saw them roar off together, from the parlor window.

"She almost knocked me down." Father brushed his mustache. "What's *that*? Brained eggs? Well."

In the afternoon, Marianne, home again, drifted about the

living room to the phonograph records. The needle hiss filled the house. She played *That Old Black Magic* twenty-one times, going "la la la" as she swam with her eyes closed, in the room.

"I'm afraid to go in my own parlor," said father. "I retired from business to smoke cigars and enjoy living, not to have a limp relative humming about under the parlor chandelier."

"Hush," said mother.

"This is a crisis," announced father, "in my life. After all, she's just visiting."

"You know how visiting girls are. Away from home they think they're in Paris, France. She'll be gone in October. It's not so dreadful."

"Let's see," figured father, slowly. "I'll have been buried just about one hundred and thirty days out at Green Lawn Cemetery by then." He got up and threw his paper down into a little white tent on the floor. "By George, Mother, I'm talking to her right *now*!"

He went and stood in the parlor door, peering through it at the waltzing Marianne. "La," she sang to the music.

Clearing his throat, he stepped through.

"Marianne," he said.

"That old black magic…" sang Marianne. "Yes?"

He watched her hands swinging in the air. She gave him a sudden fiery look as she danced by.

"I want to talk to you." He straightened his tie.

"Dah dum dee dum dum dee dum dee dum dum," she sang.

"Did you *hear* me?" he demanded.

"He's *so* nice," she said.

"Evidently."

"Do you know, he bows and opens doors like a doorman and plays a trumpet like Harry James and brought me daisies this morning?"

"I wouldn't doubt."

"His eyes are blue." She looked at the ceiling.

He could find nothing at all on the ceiling to look at.

She kept looking, as she danced, at the ceiling as he came over and stood near her, looking up, but there wasn't a rain spot or a settling crack there, and he sighed, "Marianne."

"And we ate lobster at that river café."

"Lobster. I know, but we don't want you breaking down, getting weak. One day, tomorrow, you must stay home and help your Aunt Math make her doilies—"

"Yes, sir." She dreamed around the room with her wings out.

"Did you *hear* me?" he demanded.

"Yes," she whispered. "Yes," her eyes shut. "Oh, yes, yes." Her skirts whished around. "Uncle," she said, her head back, lolling.

"You'll help your aunt with her doilies?" he cried.

"—with her doilies," she murmured.

"There!" He sat down in the kitchen, plucking up the paper. "I guess *I* told her!"

B UT, NEXT morning, he was on the edge of his bed when he heard the hot-rod's thunderous muffler and heard Marianne fall downstairs, linger two seconds in the dining room for breakfast, hesitate by the bathroom long enough to consider whether she should be sick, and then the slam of the front door, the sound of the jalopy banging down the street, two people singing off-key in it.

Father put his head in his hands. "Doilies," he said.

"What?" said mother.

"Dooley's," said father. "I'm going down to Dooley's for a morning visit."

"But Dooley's isn't open until ten."

"I'll wait," decided father, eyes shut.

That night and seven other wild nights the porch swing sang a little creaking song, back and forth, back and forth. Father, hiding in the living room, could be seen in fierce relief whenever he drafted his ten-cent cigar and the cherry light illuminated his immensely tragic face. The porch swing creaked. He waited for another creak. He heard little butterfly-soft sounds from outside, little palpitations of laughter and sweet nothings in small ears. "My porch," said father. "My swing," he whispered to his cigar, looking at it. "My house." He listened for another creak. "My lord," he said.

He went to the tool shed and appeared on the dark porch with a shiny oil-can. "No, don't get up. Don't bother. There, and there." He oiled the swing joints. It was dark. He couldn't see Marianne, he could smell her. The perfume almost knocked him off into the rosebush. He couldn't see her gentleman friend either. "Good night," he said. He went in and sat down and there was no more creaking. Now all he could hear was something that sounded like the moth-like flutter of Marianne's heart.

"He must be very nice," said mother, in the kitchen door, wiping a dinner dish.

"That's what I'm hoping," whispered father. "That's why I let them have the porch every night!"

"So many days in a row," said mother. "A girl doesn't go with a nice young man that many times unless it's serious."

"Maybe he'll propose tonight!" was father's happy thought.

"Hardly so soon. And she is so young."

"Still," he ruminated. "It might happen. It's *got* to happen, by the Lord Harry."

Grandma chuckled from her corner easy chair. It sounded like someone turning the pages of an ancient book.

"What's so funny?" said father.

"Wait and see," said grandma. "Tomorrow."

Father stared at the dark, but grandma would say no more.

"WELL, WELL," said father at breakfast. He surveyed his eggs with a kindly, paternal eye. "Well, well, by gosh, last night, on the porch, there was *more whispering*. What's his name? Isak? Well, now if I'm any judge at all, I think he proposed to Marianne last night; yes, I'm positive of it!"

"It would be nice," said mother. "A spring marriage. But it's so *soon*."

"Look," said father, with full-mouthed logic. "Marianne's the kind of girl who marries quick and young. We can't stand in her way, can we?"

"For once, I think you're right," said mother. "A marriage would be fine. Spring flowers, and Marianne looking nice in that gown I saw at Haydecker's last week."

They all peered anxiously at the stairs, waiting for Marianne to appear.

"Pardon me," rasped grandma, sighting up from her morning toast. "But I wouldn't talk of getting rid of Marianne just yet if I were you."

"And why not?"

"Because."

"Because why?"

"I hate to spoil your plans," rustled grandma, chuckling. She gestured with her little vinegary head. "But while you people were worrying about getting Marianne married, I've been keeping tab on her. Seven days now I've been watching this young fellow, each day he came in his car and honked his horn outside. He must be an actor or a quick change artist or something."

"What?" asked father.

"Yep," said grandma. "Because one day he was a young blond fellow and next day he was a tall dark fellow, and Wednesday he was a chap with a brown mustache, and Thursday he had wavy red hair, and Friday he was shorter, with a Chevrolet stripped down instead of a Ford."

Mother and father sat for a minute as if hit with hammers right behind the left ear.

At last father, his face exploding with color, shouted, "Do you mean to *say*! You *sat* there, woman, you say; all those men, and you—"

"You were always hiding." snapped grandma. "So you wouldn't spoil things. If you'd come out in the open you'd have seen the same as I. I never said a word. She'll simmer down. It's just her time of life. Every woman goes through it. It's hard, but they can survive. A new man every day does wonders for a girl's ego!"

"You, you, you, you, *you!*" Father choked on it, eyes wild, throat gorged too big for his collar. He fell back in his chair, exhausted. Mother sat, stunned.

"Good morning, everyone!" Marianne raced downstairs and popped into a chair. Father stared at her.

"You, you, you, you, you," he accused grandma.

I shall run down the street shouting, thought father wildly, and break the fire alarm window and pull the lever and bring the fire engines and the hoses. Or perhaps there will be a late snowstorm and I shall set Marianne out in it to cool.

He did neither. The heat in the room being excessive, according to the wall calendar, everyone moved out onto the cool porch while Marianne sat looking at her orange juice.

ALL ON A
SUMMER'S NIGHT

"**Y**OU'RE GETTING TOO big for this!" Grandpa gave Doug a toss toward the blazing chandelier. The boarders sat laughing, with knives and forks at hand. Then Doug, ten years old, was caught and popped in his chair and Grandma tapped his bowl with a steaming spoonful of soup. The crackers crunched like snow when he bit them. The cracker salt glittered like tiny diamonds. And there, at the far end of the table, with her gray eyes always down to watch her hand stir her coffee with a spoon or break her gingerbread and lay on the butter, was Miss Leonora Welkes, with whom men never sat on backyard swings or walked through the town ravine on summer nights. There was Miss Leonora whose eyes watched out the window as summer couples drifted by on the darkening sidewalks night after night, and Douglas felt his heart squeeze tight.

"Evening, Miss Leonora," he called.

"Evening, Douglas." She looked up past the steaming mounds of food, and the boarders turned their heads a moment before bowing again to their rituals.

Oh, Miss Welkes, he thought, Miss Welkes! And he wanted to stab every man at the table with a silver fork for not blinking their eyes at Miss Welkes when she asked for the butter. They always handed her things to their right, while still conversing with people on their left. The chandelier drew more attention than Miss Welkes. Isn't it pretty? they said. Look at it sparkle! They cried.

But they did not know Miss Welkes as he knew her. There were as many facets to her as any chandelier, and if you went about it right she could be set laughing, and it was like stirring the Chinese hanging crystals in the wind on the summer night porch, all tinkling and melody. No, Miss Welkes was cobweb and dust to them, and Douglas almost died in his chair fastening his eyes upon her all through the soup and salad.

Now the three young ladies came laughing down the stairs, late, like a troupe of orioles. They always came last to the table, as if they were actresses making entrance through the frayed blue-velvet portieres. They would hold each other by the shoulders, looking into each other's faces, telling themselves if their cheeks were pink enough or their hair ringed up tight, or their eyelashes dyed with spit-and-color enough; then they would pause, straighten their hems, and enter to something like applause from the male boarders.

"Evening, Tom, Jim, Bill. Evening, John, Peter!"

The five would tongue their food over into their cheeks, leap up, and draw out chairs for the young belles, everyone laughed until the chandelier cried with pain.

"Look what I got!"

"Look what *I* got!"

"Look at mine!"

The three ladies held up gifts which they had saved to open at table. It was the Fourth of July, and on any day of the year that was in any way special they pulled the ribbons off gifts and cried, Oh, you shouldn't have done it! They even got gifts on Memorial Day, that was how it was. Lincoln's Birthday, Washington's, Jefferson's, Columbus Day, Friday the Thirteenth. It was quite a joke. Once they got gifts on a day that wasn't any kind of day at all, with notes printed on them saying: JUST

BECAUSE IT'S *MONDAY!* They talked about that particular incident
for six months after.

Now there was a crisp rattling as they cut the ribbons with
their fingernails which flashed red, and far away at the end of the
tunnel of people sat Miss Leonora Welkes, still inching at her
food, but slowing down until at last her fork came to rest and she
watched the gifts exposed to the crystalline light.

"Perfume! With Old Glory on the box!"

"Bath powder, in the shape of a pinwheel!"

"Candy, done up in ten-inch salutes!"

Everyone said how nice it was.

Miss Leonora Welkes said, "Oh, how nice that is."

A moment later, Miss Welkes said, "I'm all done. It was a fine
meal."

"Don't you want any dessert?" asked Grandma.

"I'm choke-full." And Miss Welkes, smiling, glided from
the room.

"Smell!" cried one young lady, waving the opened perfume
under the men's noses.

"Ah! Said everyone.

Douglas hit the screen door like a bullet to a target, and before it
slammed he had taken sixty-eight steps across the cool green lawn
in his bare feet. Money jingled in his pocket, the remains of his
firecracker savings; and quite a remains, too. Now he thudded his
bare feet on the warm summer twilight cement, across the street to
press his nose on Mrs.Singer's store window, to see the devils laid in
red round rows, the torpedoes in sawdust, the ten-inch salutes that
could toss your head in the trees like a football, the nine inchers
that could bang a can to the sun, and the fire balloons, so rare
and beautiful, like withered red, white and blue butterflies, their
delicate silk wings folded, ready to be lit and gassed with warm air
later and sent up into the summer night among the stars. There
were so many things to pack your pocket with, and yet as he stood
there, counting the money, ten, twenty, forty, a dollar and seventy
cents, precariously saved during a long year of mowing lawns and

clipping hedges, he turned and looked back at Grandma's house, at the highest room of all, up in the little green cupola, where the window was shut in the hottest weather, and the shades half drawn. Miss Welkes' room.

In half an hour the kids would come like a summer shower, their feet raining on the pavement, their hands full of explosions, little adhesive turbans on their burned thumbs, smelling of brimstone and punk, to run him off in fairy circles where they waved the magical sparklers, tracing their names and their destinies in luminous firefly paths on the sultry evening air, making great white symbols that lingered in phosphorous after-image even if you looked down from your night bed at three in the morning, remembering what a day and what an evening it had been. In half an hour he would be fat with treasure, breast pockets bulging with torpedoes, his money gone. But—now. He looked back and forth between the high room in Grandma's house, and this store window full of dynamite wonders.

How many nights in winter had he gone down to the stone public library and seen Miss Welkes there with the stamp pad at her elbow and the purple ink rubber stamper in her hand, and the great book sections behind her?

"Good evening, Douglas."

"Evening, Miss Welkes."

"Can I help you meet some new friend, tonight?"

"Yes'm."

"I know a man named Longfellow," she said. Or, "I know a man named Whittier."

And that was it. It wasn't so much Miss Welkes herself, it was the people she knew. On autumn nights when, for no reason, the library might be empty for hours on end, she would say, "Let me bring out Mr. Whittier." And she went back among the warm stacks of books, and returned to sit under the green glass shade, opening the book to meet the season, while Douglas sat on a stool looking up as her lips moved and, half of the time, she didn't even glance at the words but could look away or close her eyes while she recited the poem about the pumpkin:

Oh—fruit loved of childhood—the old days recalling,
  When wood grapes were purpling and brown nuts were falling!
When wild ugly faces we carved in its skin,
  Glaring out through the dark with a candle within!

And Douglas would walk home, tall and enchanted.

Or on silver winter evenings when he and the wind blew wide the library door and dust stirred on the farthest counters and magazines turned their pages unaided in the vast empty rooms, then what more particularly apt than a good friend of Miss Welkes? Mr. Robert Frost, what a name for winter! His poem about stopping by the woods on a winter evening to watch the woods fill up with snow....

And in the summer, only last night, Mr. Whittier again, on a hot night in July that kept the people at home lying on their porches, the library like a great bread oven; there, under the green grass lamp:

Blessings on thee, little man,
  Barefoot boy with cheeks of tan...
Every morn shall lead thee through,
  Fresh baptisms of the dew!

And Miss Welkes' face there, an oval with her cobweb graying hair and her plainness, would be enchanted, color risen to her cheeks, and wetness to her lips, and the light from the reflection on the book pages shining her eyes and coloring her hair to a brightness!

In winter, he trudged home through icelands of magic, in summer through bakery winds of sorcery; the seasons given substance by the readings of Miss Welkes who knew so many people and introduced them, in due time, to Douglas. Mr. Poe and Mr. Sandburg and Miss Amy Lowell and Mr. Shakespeare.

The screen door opened under his hand.

"Mrs. Singer," he said, "have you got any perfume?"

THE GIFT lay at the top of the stairs, tilted against her door. Supper had been early, over at six o'clock. There was the warm lull now before the extravagant evening. Downstairs, you could hear the tinkling of plates lifted to their kitchen wall racks. Douglas, at the furthest bend of the stairs, half hid in the attic door shadows, waited for Miss Welkes to twist her brass doorknob, waited to see the gift drop at her feet, unsigned, anonymous, sparkling with tape and gold stars.

At last, the door opened. The gift fell.

Miss Welkes looked down at it as if she was standing on the edge of a cliff she had never guessed was there before. She looked in all directions, slowly, and bent to pick it up. She didn't open it, but stood in the doorway, holding the gift in her hands, for a long time. He heard her move inside and set the gift on a table. But there was no rattle of paper. She was looking at the gift, the wrapping, the tape, the stars, and not touching it.

"Oh, Miss Welkes, Miss Welkes!" he wanted to cry.

Half an hour later, there she was, on the front porch, seated with her neat hands folded, and watching the door. It was the summer evening ritual, the people on the porches, in the swings, on the figured pillows, the women talking and sewing, the men smoking, the children in idle groupings on the steps. But this was early, the town porches still simmering from the day, the echoes only temporarily allayed, the civil war of Independence Afternoon muffled for an hour in the sounds of poured lemonade and scraped dishes. But here, the only person on the street porches, alone, was Miss Eleanora Welkes, her face pink instead of gray, flushed, her eyes watching the door, her body tensed forward. Douglas saw her from the tree where he hung in silent vigilance. He did not say hello, she did not see him there, and the hour passed into deeper twilight. Within the house the sounds of preparation grew intense and furious. Phones rang, feet ran up and down the avalanche of stairs, the three belles giggled, bath doors slammed, and then out and down the front steps went the three young ladies, one at a time, a man on her arm. Each time the door swung, Miss Welkes would lean forward, smiling wildly. And each time she sank back as the girls appeared in floaty green dresses and blew away like thistle down the darkening avenues, laughing up at the men.

That left only Mr. Britz and Mr. Jerrick, who lived upstairs across from Miss Welkes. You could hear them whistling idly at their mirrors, and through the open windows you could see them finger their ties.

Miss Welkes leaned over the porch geraniums to peer up at their windows, her heart pumping in her face, it seemed, making it heart-shaped and colorful. She was looking for the man who had left the gift.

And then Douglas smelled the odor. He almost fell from the tree.

Miss Welkes had tapped her ears and neck with drops of perfume, many, many bright drops of *Summer Night Odor*, 97 cents a bottle! And she was sitting where the warm wind might blow this scent to whoever stepped out upon the porch. This would be her way of saying, I got your gift! *Well?*

"It was me, Miss Welkes!" screamed Douglas, silently, and hung in the tree, cold as ice.

"Good evening, Mr. Jerrick," said Miss Welkes, half-rising.

"Evening." Mr. Jerrick sniffed in the doorway and looked at her. "Have a nice evening." He went whistling down the steps.

That left only Mr. Britz, with his straw hat cocked over one eye, humming.

"Here I am," said Miss Welkes, rising, certain that this must be the man, the last one in the house.

"There you are," said Mr. Britz, blinking. "Hey, you smell good. I never knew you used scent." He leered at her.

"Someone gave me a gift."

"Well, that's fine." And Mr. Britz did a little dance going down the porch steps, his cane jauntily flung over his shoulder. "See you later, Miss W." He marched off.

Miss Welkes sat, and Douglas hung in the cooling tree. The kitchen sounds were fading. In a moment, Grandma would come out, bringing her pillow and a bottle of mosquito oil. Grandpa would cut the end off a long stogie and puff it to kill his own particular insects, and the aunts and uncles would arrive for the Independence Evening Event at the Spaulding House, the Festival of Fire, the shooting stars, the Roman Candles so diligently held by Grandpa, looking like Julius Caesar gone to flesh, standing with great dignity on the dark summer lawn, directing the setting off of fountains of red fire, and pinwheels of sizzle and smoke, while everyone, as if to the order of some celestial doctor, opened their mouths and said Ah! their faces burned into quick colors by blue, red, yellow, white flashes of sky bomb among the cloudy stars. The house windows would jingle with concussion. And Miss Welkes would sit among the strange people, the scent of perfume evaporating during the evening hours, until it was gone, and only the sad, wet smell of punk and sulfur would remain.

THE CHILDREN screamed by on the dim street now, calling for Douglas, but, hidden, he did not answer. He felt in his pocket for the remaining dollar and fifty cents. The children ran away into the night.

Douglas swung and dropped. He stood by the porch steps.

"Miss Welkes?"

She glanced up. "Yes?"

Now that the time had come he was afraid. Suppose she refused, suppose she was embarrassed and ran up to lock her door and never came out again?

"Tonight," he said, "there's a swell show at the Elite Theater. Harold Lloyd in *WELCOME, DANGER*. The show starts at eight o'clock, and afterward we'll have a chocolate sundae at the Midnight Drug Store, open until eleven forty-five. I'll go change clothes."

She looked down at him and didn't speak. Then she opened the door and went up the stairs.

"Miss Welkes!" he cried.

"It's all right," she said. "Run and put your shoes on!"

I T WAS seven thirty, the porch filling with people, when Douglas emerged, in his dark suit, with a blue tie, his hair wet with water, and his feet in the hot tight shoes.

"Why, Douglas!" the aunts and uncles and Grandma and Grandpa cried, "Aren't you staying for the fireworks?"

"No." And he looked at the fireworks laid out so beautifully crisp and smelling of powder, the pinwheels and sky bombs, and the Fire Balloons, three of them, folded like moths in their tissue wings, those balloons he loved most dearly of all, for they were like a summer night dream going up quietly, breathlessly on the still high air, away and away to far lands, glowing and breathing light as long as you could see them. Yes, the Fire Balloons, those especially would he miss, while seated in the Elite Theater tonight.

There was a whisper, the screen door stood wide, and there was Miss Welkes.

"Good evening, Mr. Spaulding," she said to Douglas.

"Good evening, Miss Welkes," he said.

She was dressed in a gray suit no one had seen ever before, neat and fresh, with her hair up under a summer straw hat, and standing there in the dim porch light she was like the carved goddess on the great marble library clock come to life.

"Shall we go, Mr. Spaulding?" and Douglas walked her down the steps.

"Have a good time!" said everyone.

"Douglas!" called Grandfather.

"Yes, sir?"

"Douglas," said Grandfather, after a pause, holding his cigar in his hand, "I'm saving one of the Fire Balloons. I'll be up when you come home. We'll light her together and send her up. How's that sound, eh?"

"Swell!" said Douglas.

"Good night, boy." Grandpa waved him quietly on.

"Good night, sir."

He took Miss Eleanora Welkes down the street, over the sidewalks of the summer evening, and they talked about Mr. Longfellow and Mr. Whittier and Mr. Poe all the way to the Elite Theater....

MISS BIDWELL

OLD MISS BIDWELL used to sit with a lemonade glass in her hand in her squeaking rocker on the porch of her house on Saint James Street every summer night from seven until nine. At nine, you could hear the front door tap shut, the brass key turn in the lock, the shades rustle down, and the lights click out.

Her routine varied in no detail. She lived alone with a house full of rococo pictures, a dusty library, a yellow-mouthed piano, and a music box which, when she ratcheted it up and set it going, prickled the air like the bubbles from lemon soda pop. Miss Bidwell had a nod for everyone walking by, and it was interesting that her house had no front steps leading up to its wooden porch. No front steps, and no back steps, for Miss Bidwell hadn't left her house in forty years. In the year 1909, she had had the back and the front steps completely torn down and the porches railed in.

In the autumn—the closing-up, the nailing-in, the hiding-away time—she would have one last lemonade on her cooling, bleak porch; then she would carry her wicker chair inside, and no one would see her again until the next spring.

"There she goes," said Mr. Widmer, the grocer, pointing with the red apple in his hand. "Take a good look at her." He tapped the wall calendar. "Nine o'clock of an evening in the month of September, the day after Labor Day."

Several customers squinted over at Miss Bidwell's house. There was the old lady, looking around for a final time; then she went inside.

"Won't see her again until May first," said Mr. Widmer. "There's a trap door in her kitchen wall. I unlock that trap door and shove the groceries in. There's an envelope there, with money in it and a list of the things she wants. I never see her."

"What does she do all winter?"

"Only the Lord knows. She's had a phone for forty years and never used it."

Miss Bidwell's house was dark.

Mr. Widmer bit into his apple, enjoying its crisp succulence. "Forty years ago, she had the front steps taken away."

"Why? Folks die?"

"They died before that."

"Husband or children die?"

"Never had no husband nor children. She held hands with a young man who had all kinds of notions about travelling. They were going to be married. He used to sit and play the guitar and sing to her on that porch. One day he just went to the rail station and bought one ticket for Arizona, California, and China."

"That's a long time for a woman to carry a torch."

They laughed quietly and solemnly, for it was a sad admission they had made.

"Suppose she'll *ever* come out?"

"When you're *seventy*? All I do every year is wait for the first of May. If she don't come out on the porch that day and set up her chair, I'll know for sure she's dead. Then I'll phone the police."

"Goodnight," said everyone, and left Mr. Widmer alone in the gray light of his grocery shop.

Mr. Widmer put on his coat and listened to the whining of the wind grow stronger. Yes, every year. And every year at this time he'd watched the old woman become more of an old woman. She was as remote as one of those barometers where the woman comes out for fair weather, the man appears for bad. But what a broken instrument, with only the woman coming out and coming out alone, and never a man at all, for bad or for better. How many thousands of July and August nights had he seen her there, beyond her moat of green grass, which was as impassable as a crocodile stream? Forty years of small-town nights. How much might they weigh if put to the scale? A feather to himself, but how much to *her*?

Mr. Widmer was putting on his hat when he saw the man.

The man came along the street, on the other side; an old man, dim in the light of the single corner street lamp. He was looking at all the house numbers, and when he came to the corner house, Number 11, he stopped and looked at the light-less windows.

"It couldn't be," said Mr. Widmer. He turned out the light and stood in the warm grocery smell of his store, watching the old man through the plate glass. "Not after this much time." He shook his head. It was much more than ridiculous, for hadn't he felt his heart quicken at least once a day, every day, for four decades whenever he saw a man pass or pause by Miss Bidwell's? Every man in the history of the town who had so much as tied a shoelace in front of her locked house had been a source of wonder to Mr. Widmer.

"Are *you* the young man who ran off and left our Miss Bidwell?" he cried aloud, to himself.

Once, thirty years ago, white apron flapping, he had run across the brick street to confront a young man. "Well, so you came back!"

"What?" the young man said.

"Aren't you Mr. Robert Farr, the one who brought her red carnations and played the guitar, and sang?"

"The name's Corley," and the young man drew forth silk samples to display and sell.

A S THE years passed, Mr. Widmer had become frightened about one thing: Suppose Mr. Farr *did* come back some day—how was he to be recognized? In his mind Mr. Widmer remembered the man as striding and young and very clean-faced. But forty years could peel a man away and dry his bones and tighten his flesh into a fine, acid etching. Perhaps some day Mr. Farr might return, like a hound dog to old trails, and, because of Mr. Widmer's negligence, think the house locked and buried deep in another century, and go on down the avenue, never the wiser. Perhaps it had happened *already*!

There stood the man, the old man, the unbelievable man, at nine-fifteen in the evening of the day after Labor Day in September. There was a slight bend to his knees and his back, and his face was turned to the Bidwell house.

"One last try," said Mr. Widmer. "Sticking my nose in."

He stepped lightly over the cool brick street and reached the farther curb. The old man turned toward him.

"Evening," said Mr. Widmer.

"I wonder if you could help me?" said the old man. "Is this the old Bidwell house?"

"Yes."

"Does anyone live there?"

"Miss Ann Bidwell, she's still there."

"Thank you."

"Goodnight." And Mr. Widmer walked off, his heart pounding, cursing himself. Why didn't you ask him, you idiot! Why didn't you say, Mr. Farr? Is that you Mr. Farr?

But he knew the answer. This time, he wanted it to *be* Mr. Farr. And the only way to insure that it *was* Mr. Farr was not to shatter the thin bubble of reality. Asking outright might have evoked an answer which would have crushed him all over again. No, I'm not Mr. Farr; no, I'm not him. But *this* way, by *not* asking, Mr. Widmer could go to his home tonight, could lie in his upstairs bed, and, for an hour or so, could imagine, with an ancient and implausible tinge of romanticism, that at last the wandering man had come home from long track ways of travelling and long years of other cities and other worlds. This sort of lie was the most pleasant in which to indulge. You don't ask a dream if it is real, or you wake up. All right then, let that man—bill collector, trash man, or whatever—for this night, at least, assume the identity of a lost person.

Mr. Widmer walked back across the street, around the side of his store, and up the narrow, dark stairs to the second floor where his wife was already in bed, asleep.

"Suppose it *is* him," he thought, in bed. "And he's knocking on the house sides, knocking on the back door with a broom handle, tapping at the windows, calling her on the phone, leaving his card poked under the doors—suppose?"

He turned on his side.

Will she answer? He wondered. Will she pay attention, will she do anything? Or will she just sit in her house with the fenced-in porch and no steps going up or down to the door, and let him knock and call her name?

He turned on his other side.

Will we see her again next May first, and not until then? And will he wait until then…six months of knocking and calling her name and waiting?

He got up and went to the window. There, far away over the green lawns, at the base of the huge, black house, by the porch which had no steps, stood the old man. And was it imagination or was his voice calling, calling there under the autumn trees, at the lightless windows?

THE NEXT morning, very early, Mr. Widmer looked down at Miss Bidwell's lawn.

It was empty. "I doubt if he was even there," said Mr. Widmer. "I doubt I even talked to anyone but a lamp-post. That apple was half cider; it turned my head."

It was seven o'clock. Mrs. Terle and Mrs. Adams came into the cold store for bacon and eggs and milk. Mr. Widmer edged around the subject. "Say, you didn't see no prowlers near Miss Bidwell's last night, did you?"

"Were there some?" cried the ladies.

"Thought I saw some."

"I didn't see no one," they said.

"It was the apple," murmured Mr. Widmer. "Pure cider."

The door slammed, and Mr. Widmer felt his spirits slump. Only he had seen, and the seeing must have been the rusted product of too many years of trying to live out another person's life.

The streets were empty, but the town was slowly arising to life. The sun was a reddish ball over the Court House Clock. Dew still lay on everything in a cool blanket. Dew stood in bubbles on every grass blade, on every silent red brick; dripped from the elms and the maples and the empty apple trees.

The dew.

He walked slowly and carefully across the empty street and stood on Miss Bidwell's sidewalk. Her lawns, a vast green sea of dew that had fallen in the night, lay before him. Mr. Widmer felt again the warm pounding of his heart. For there, in the dew, circling and circling the house, where they had left fine, clear impressions, was a series of endless footprints, around and around, under the windows, near the bushes, at the doors. Footprints in the crystal grass, footprints that melted as the sun rose.

The day was a slow day. Mr. Widmer kept near the front of his store, but saw nothing. At sunset, he sat smoking under the store awning. Maybe he's gone, maybe he'll never come back. She didn't answer. I know her. She's old and proud. The older, the prouder, that's what they say. Maybe he's gone off on the train again. Why didn't I ask his name? Why didn't I pound on the doors *with* him!

But the fact remained that he hadn't asked and he hadn't pounded, and he felt himself the nucleus of a tragedy that was beginning to grow far beyond him.

He won't come back. Not after all night walking around her house. He must have left just before dawn. Footsteps still fresh.

Eight o'clock. Eight-thirty. Nothing. Nine o'clock. Nine-thirty. Nothing. Mr. Widmer stayed open until quite late, even though there were no customers.

It was after eleven when he sat by the upstairs window of his home, not watching exactly, but not going to bed, either.

At eleven-thirty, the clock struck softly, and the old man came along the street and stood before the house.

Of course! Said Mr. Widmer to himself. He's afraid someone will see him. He slept all day somewhere and waited. Afraid of what people might say. Look at him there, going around and around.

He listened.

There was the calling again. Like the last cricket of the year, like the last rustle of the last oak leaf of the season. At the front door, at the back, at the bay windows. Oh, there would be a million slow footprints in the meadow lawn tomorrow when the sun rose.

Was she *listening*?

"Ann, Ann, oh, Ann!" Was that what he called? "Ann, can you hear me, Ann?" Was that what you called when you came back very late in the day?

And then, suddenly, Mr. Widmer stood up.

SUPPOSE SHE didn't *hear* him! How could he be sure she was still *able* to hear? Seventy years make for spider webs in the ears, gray waddings of time which dull everything for some people until they live in a universe of cotton and wool and silence. Nobody had spoken to her in thirty years, save to open their mouths to say hello. What if she were deaf, lying there in her cold bed now like a little girl playing out a long and lonely game, never even aware someone was calling through her flake-painted door, someone was walking on the soft grass around her locked house? Perhaps not pride but a physical inability prevented her from answering!

In the living room, Mr. Widmer quietly took the phone off the hook, watching the bedroom door to be certain he hadn't wakened his wife. To the operator he said, "Helen? Give me 729."

"That you, Mr. Widmer? Funny time of night to *call* her."

"Never mind."

"All right, but she won't answer. Never has. Don't recall she ever *has* used her phone in all the years after she had it put in."

The phone rang. It rang six times, and nothing happened.

"Keep trying, Helen."

The phone rang twelve times more. His face was streaming perspiration. Someone picked up the phone at the other end.

"Miss Bidwell!" cried Mr. Widmer, almost collapsing in relief. "Miss Bidwell?" he lowered his voice. "This is Mr. Widmer, the grocer, calling."

No answer. She was on the other end, in her house, standing in the dark. Through his window he could see that her house was still unlit. She hadn't switched on any lights to find the phone.

"Miss Bidwell, do you hear me?" he asked.

Silence.

"Miss Bidwell, I want you to do me a favor," he said.

Click.

"I want you to open your front door and look out," he said.

"She's hung up," said Helen. "Want me to call her again?"

"No thanks."

He put the receiver back on the hook.

There was the house, in the morning sun, in the afternoon sun, and in the twilight—silent. Here was the grocery, with Mr. Widmer in it, thinking: She's a fool. No matter what, she's a fool! It's never too late. No matter how old, wrinkled hands are better than none. He's travelled a long way around, and by his look, he's never married, but always travelled, as some men do, crazy to change their scenery every week, every month, every year, until they reach an age where they find they are collecting nothing at all but a lot of empty trips and a lot of towns with no more substance to them than movie sets and a lot of people in those towns who are about as real as wax dummies seen in lighted windows late at night as you pass by on a slow, black train. He's been living with a world of people who didn't care about him because he never stayed anywhere long enough to make anyone worry whether he would arise in the morning or whether he had turned to dust. And then he got to thinking about "her" and decided she was the one real person he'd ever known. And just a little too late, he took a train and got off and walked up here, and there he is on her lawn, feeling like a fool, and one more night of this and he won't come back at all.

This was the third night. Mr. Widmer thought of going over, of breaking the glass in the firebox, of setting fire to the porch of Miss Bidwell's house, and of causing the firemen to roar up. That would bring her out, right into the old man's arms, by Jupiter!

But wait! Ah, but wait.

Mr. Widmer's eyes went to the ceiling. Up there, in the attic—wasn't there a weapon there to be used against pride and time? In all that dust, wasn't there something with which to strike out? Something as old as all of them—Mr. Widmer, the old man, the old lady? How long since the attic has been cleaned out? Never.

But it was too ridiculous. He wouldn't dare!

And yet, this was the last night. A weapon *must* be provided.

Ten minutes later, he heard his wife cry out to him:

"Tom, Tom! What's that noise! What are you doing in the attic?"

A T ELEVEN-THIRTY, there was the old man. He stood in front of the step-less house, as if not knowing what to try next. And then he took a quick step and looked down.

Mr. Widmer, from his upstairs window, whispered, "Yes, yes, go ahead."

The old man bent over.

"Pick it up!" cried Mr. Widmer.

The old man extended his hands.

"Brush it off! I know, I know it's dusty. But it's still fair enough. Brush it *off*, use it!"

In the moonlight, the old man held a guitar in his hands. It had been lying in the middle of the lawn. There was a period of long waiting during which the old man turned it over with his fingers.

"Go on!" said Mr. Widmer.

There was a tentative chord of music.

"Go on!" said Mr. Widmer. "What voices can't do, music can. That's it! Play! You're right, try it!" urged Mr. Widmer. And he thought: Sing under the windows, sing under the apple trees and near the back porch, sing until the guitar notes shake her, sing until she starts to cry. You get a woman to crying, and you're on safe ground. Her pride will all wash away; and the best thing to start the dissolving and crying is music. Sing songs, sing "Genevieve, Sweet Genevieve, the years may come, the years may go," and sing "Meet Me Tonight in Dreamland," and sing "We were Sailing Along on Moonlight Bay," and sing "There's a Long, Long Trail Awinding," and sing all those old summer songs and old-time songs, any song that's old and quiet and lovely; do that, and keep on doing that; sing soft and light, with a few notes of the guitar; sing and play and perhaps you'll hear the key turn in the lock!

He listened.

As pure as drops of water falling in the night, the guitar played, soft, soft, and it was half an hour before the old man began to sing, and it was so faint no one could hear; no one except someone behind a wall in that house, in a bed, or standing in the dark behind a shaded window.

Mr. Widmer went to bed, numb, and lay there for an hour, hearing the faraway guitar.

THE NEXT morning, Mrs. Terle said, "I seen that prowler."

"Yes?"

"He was there all night. Playing a guitar. Can you imagine? How silly can old people get? Who is he, anyway?"

"I'm sure I don't know," said Mr. Widmer.

"Well, him and his guitar went away down the street at six this morning," said Mrs. Terle.

"Did he? Didn't he come back?"

"No."

"Didn't the door open for him?"

"No. Should it?"

"I suppose not. He'll be back tonight."

She went out.

Tonight will do it, thought Mr. Widmer. Tonight, just one more night. He's not the sort to give up now. Now that he has the guitar, he'll be back, and tonight will do it. Mr. Widmer whistled, moving about the store.

A truck drove up outside the store, and Mr. Frank Henderson climbed out, a kit of hammers and nails and a saw in his hands. He went around behind the truck and took out a couple of dozen fresh-cut, new pieces of raw, good-smelling lumber.

"Morning, Frank," called Mr. Widmer. "How's the carpentry business?"

"Picking up this morning," said Frank. He sorted out the good, yellow lumber and the bright steel nails. "Got a job."

"Where?"

"Miss Bidwell's."

"Yes?" Mr. Widmer felt his heart begin the familiar pounding.

"Yes. She phoned an hour ago. Wants me to build a new set of steps onto her front porch. Wants it done today."

Mr. Widmer stood looking at the carpenter's hands, at the hammer and nails, and the good fresh clean lumber. The sun was rising higher every minute now and the day was bright.

"Here," said Mr. Widmer, picking up some of the wood. "Let me help."

They walked across the brick street and over the lawn of Miss Bidwell's house together, carrying the planks and the saw and the nails.

❀

THE PUMPERNICKEL

MR. AND MRS. Welles walked away from the movie theater late at night and went into the quiet little store, a combination restaurant and delicatessen. They settled in a booth, and Mrs. Welles said, "Baked ham on pumpernickel." Mr. Welles glanced toward the counter and there lay a loaf of pumpernickel.

"Why," he murmured, "pumpernickel...Druce's Lake..."

The night, the late hour, the empty restaurant—by now the pattern was familiar. Anything could set him off on a tide of reminiscence. The scent of autumn leaves, or midnight winds blowing, could stir him from himself, and memories would pour around him. Now in the unreal hour after the theater, in this lonely store, he saw a loaf of pumpernickel bread and, as on a thousand other nights, he found himself moved into the past.

"Druce's Lake," he said again.

"What?" His wife glanced up.

"Something I'd almost forgotten," said Mr. Welles. "In 1910, when I was twenty, I nailed a loaf of pumpernickel to the top of my bureau mirror..."

In the hard, shiny crust of the bread, the boys at Druce's Lake had cut their names: *Tom, Nick, Bill, Alec, Paul, Jack.* The finest picnic in history! Their faces tanned as they rattled down the dusty roads. Those were the days when roads were *really* dusty; a fine brown talcum floured up after your car. And the lake was always twice as good to reach as it would be later in life when you arrived immaculate, clean and unrumpled.

"That was the last time the old gang got together." Mr. Welles said.

After that, college, work and marriage separated you. Suddenly you found yourself with some other group. And you never felt as comfortable or as much at ease again in all your life.

"I wonder," said Mr. Welles. "I like to think maybe we all *knew*, somehow, that this picnic might be the last we'd have. You first get that empty feeling the day after high-school graduation. Then, when a little time passes and no one vanished immediately, you relax. But after a year you realize the old world is changing. And you want to do some one last thing before you lose one another. While you're all still friends, home from college for the summer, this side of marriage, you've got to have something like a last ride and a swim in the cool lake."

Mr. Welles remembered that rare summer morning, he and Tom lying under his father's Ford, reaching up their hands to adjust this or that, talking about machines and women and the future. While they worked, that day got warm. At last Tom said, "Why don't we drive out to Druce's Lake?"

As simple as that.

Yet forty years later, you remember every detail of picking up the other fellows, everyone yelling under the green trees.

"Hey!" Alec beating everyone's head with the pumpernickel and laughing. "This is for extra sandwiches, later."

Nick had made the sandwiches that were already in the hamper—the garlic kind they would eat less of as the years passed and the girls moved in.

Then, squeezing three in the front, three in the rear, with their arms across one another's shoulders, they drove through the boiling, dusty countryside, with a cake of ice in a tin washtub to cool the beer they'd buy.

What was the special quality of that day that it should focus like a stereoscopic image, fresh and clear, forty years later? Perhaps each of them had an experience like his own. A few days before the picnic, he had found a photograph of his father twenty-five years younger, standing with a group of friends at college. The photograph had disturbed him, made him aware as he had not been before of the passing of time, the swift flow of the years away from youth. A picture taken of him as he was now would, in twenty-five years, look as strange to his own children as his father's picture did to him—unbelievably young, a stranger out of a strange, never-returning time.

Was that how the final picnic had come about—with each of them knowing that in a few short years they would be crossing streets to avoid one another, or, if they met, saying, "We've *got* to have lunch sometime!" but never doing it? Whatever the reason, Mr. Welles could still hear the splashes as they'd plunged off the pier under a yellow sun. And then the beer and sandwiches underneath the shady trees.

We never ate that pumpernickel, Mr. Welles thought. Funny, if we'd been a bit hungrier, we'd have cut it up, and I wouldn't have been reminded of it by that loaf there on the counter.

Lying under the trees in a golden peace that came from beer and sun and male companionship, they promised that in ten years they would meet at the courthouse on New Year's Day, 1920, to see what they had done with their lives. Talking their rough easy talk, they carved their names in the pumpernickel.

"Driving home," Mr. Welles said, "we sang 'Moonlight Bay'."

He remembered motoring along in the hot, dry night with their swim suits damp on the jolting floor boards. It was a ride of many detours taken just for the hell of it, which was the best reason in the world.

"Good night." "So long." "Good night."

Then Welles was driving alone, at midnight, home to bed.

He nailed the pumpernickel to his bureau the next day.

"I almost cried when, two years later, my mother threw it in the incinerator while I was off at college."

"What happened in 1920?" asked his wife. "On New Year's Day?"

"Oh," said Mr. Welles. "I was walking by the courthouse, by accident, at noon. It was snowing. I heard the clock strike. Lord, I thought, we were supposed to meet here today! I waited five minutes. Not right in front of the courthouse, no. I waited across the street." He paused. "Nobody showed up."

He got up from the table and paid the bill. "And I'll take that loaf of unsliced pumpernickel there," he said.

When he and his wife were walking home, he said, "I've got a crazy idea. I often wondered what happened to everyone."

"Nick's still in town with his café."

"But what about the others?" Mr. Welles's face was getting pink and he was smiling and waving his hands. "They moved away. I think Tom's in Cincinnati. He looked quickly at his wife. "Just for the heck of it, I'll send him this pumpernickel!"

"Oh, but—"

"Sure!" He laughed, walking faster, slapping the bread with the palm of his hand. "Have him carve his name on it and mail it on to the others if he knows their addresses. And finally back to me, with all their names on it!"

"But," she said, taking his arm, "it'll only make you unhappy. You've done things like this so many times before and…"

He wasn't listening. Why do I never get these ideas by day? He thought. Why do I always get them after the sun goes down?

In the morning, first thing, he thought, I'll mail this pumpernickel off, by God, to Tom and the others. And when it comes back I'll have the loaf just as it was when it got thrown out and burned! Why not?

"Let's see," he said, as his wife opened the screen door and let him into the stuffy-smelling house to be greeted by silence and warm emptiness. "Let's see. We also sang 'Row Row Row Your Boat,' didn't we?"

IN THE morning, he came down the hall stairs and paused a moment in the strong full sunlight, his face shaved, his teeth freshly brushed. Sunlight brightened every room. He looked in at the breakfast table.

His wife was busy there. Slowly, calmly, she was slicing the pumpernickel.

He sat down at the table in the warm sunlight and reached for the newspaper.

She picked up a slice of the newly cut bread, and kissed him on the cheek. He patted her arm.

"One or two pieces of toast, dear?" she asked gently.

"Two, I think," he replied.

THE SCREAMING WOMAN

MY NAME IS Margaret Leary and I'm ten years old and in the fifth grade at Central School. I haven't any brothers or sisters, but I've got a nice father and mother except they don't pay much attention to me. And anyway, we never thought we'd have anything to do with a murdered woman. Or almost, anyway.

When you're just living on a street like we live on, you don't think awful things are going to happen, like shooting or stabbing or burying people under the ground, practically in your back yard. And when it does happen you don't believe it. You just go on buttering your toast or baking a cake.

I got to tell you how it happened. It was a noon in the middle of July. It was hot and Mama said to me, "Margaret, you go to the store and buy some ice cream. It's Saturday, Dad's home for lunch, so we'll have a treat."

I ran out across the empty lot behind our house. It was a big lot, where kids had played baseball, and broken glass and stuff. And on my way back from the store with the ice cream I was just walking along, minding my own business, when all of a sudden it happened.

I heard the Screaming Woman.

I stopped and listened.

It was coming up out of the ground.

A woman was buried under the rocks and dirt and glass, and she was screaming, all wild and horrible, for someone to dig her out.

I just stood there, afraid. She kept screaming, muffled.

Then I started to run. I fell down, got up, and ran some more. I got in the screen door of my house and there was Mama, calm as you please, not knowing what I knew, that there was a real live woman buried out in back of our house, just a hundred yards away, screaming bloody murder.

"Mama," I said.

"Don't stand there with the ice cream," said Mama.

"But, Mama," I said.

"Put it in the icebox," she said.

"Listen, Mama, there's a Screaming Woman in the empty lot."

"And wash your hands," said Mama.

"She was screamin' and screamin'..."

"Let's see now, salt and pepper," said Mama, far away.

"Listen to me," I said, loud. "We got to dig her out. She's buried under tons and tons of dirt and if we don't dig her out, she'll choke up and die."

"I'm certain she can wait until after lunch," said Mama.

"Mama, don't you believe me?"

"Of course, dear. Now wash your hands and take this plate of meat in to your father."

"I don't even know who she is or how she got there," I said. "But we got to help her before it's too late."

"Good gosh," said Mama. "Look at this ice cream. What did you do, just stand in the sun and let it melt?"

"Well, the empty lot..."

"Go on, now, scoot."

I went into the dining room.

"Hi, Dad, there's a Screaming Woman in the empty lot."

"I never knew a woman who didn't," said Dad.

"I'm serious," I said.

"You look very grave," said Father.

"We've got to get picks and shovels and excavate, like for an Egyptian mummy," I said.

"I don't feel like an archaeologist, Margaret," said Father. "Now, some nice cool October day, I'll take you up on that."

"But we can't wait that long," I almost screamed. My heart was bursting in me. I was excited and scared and afraid and here was Dad, putting meat on his plate, cutting and chewing and paying me no attention.

"Dad?" I said.

"Mmmm?" he said, chewing.

"Dad, you just gotta come out after lunch and help me," I said. "Dad, Dad, I'll give you all the money in my piggy bank!"

"Well," said Dad, "so it's a business proposition, is it? It must be important for you to offer your perfectly good money. How much money will you pay, by the hour?"

"I got five whole dollars it took me a year to save, and it's all yours."

Dad touched my arm. "I'm touched. I'm really touched. You want me to play with you and you're willing to pay for my time. Honest, Margaret, you make your old Dad feel like a piker. I don't give you enough time. Tell you what, after lunch, I'll come out and listen to your screaming woman, free of charge."

"Will you, oh, will you, really?"

"Yes, ma'am, that's what I'll do," said Dad. "But you must promise me one thing?"

"What?"

"If I come out, you must eat all of your lunch first."

"I promise," I said.

"Okay."

Mother came in and sat down and we started to eat.

"Not so fast," said Mama.

I slowed down. Then I started eating fast again.

"You heard your mother," said Dad.

"The Screaming Woman," I said. "We got to hurry."

"I," said Father, "intend sitting here quietly and judiciously giving my attention first to my steak, then to my potatoes, and my salad, of course, and then to my ice cream, and after that to a long drink of iced coffee, if you don't mind. I may be a good hour at it. And another thing, young lady, if you mention her name, this Screaming What-sis, once more at this table during lunch, I won't go out with you to hear her recital."

"Yes, sir."

"Is that understood?"

"Yes, sir," I said.

Lunch was a million years long. Everybody moved in slow motion, like those films you see at the movies. Mama got up slow and got down slow and forks and knives and spoons moved slow. Even the flies in the room were slow. And Dad's cheek muscles moved slow. It was so slow. I wanted to scream, "Hurry! Oh, please, rush, get up, run around, come on out, run!"

But no, I had to sit, and all the while we sat there slowly, slowly eating our lunch, out there in the empty lot (I could hear her screaming in my mind. *Scream!*) was the Screaming Woman, all alone, while the world ate its lunch and the sun was hot and the lot was empty as the sky.

"There we are," said Dad, finished at last.

"Now will you come out to see the Screaming Woman?" I said.

"First a little more iced coffee," said Dad.

"Speaking of Screaming Women," said Mother, "Charlie Nesbitt and his wife Helen had another fight last night."

"That's nothing new," said Father. "They're always fighting."

"If you ask me, Charlie's no good," said Mother. "Or her, either."

"Oh, I don't know," said Dad. "I think she's pretty nice."

"You're prejudiced. After all, you almost married her."

"You going to bring that up again?" he said. "After all, I was only engaged to her six weeks."

"You showed some sense when you broke it off."

"Oh, you know Helen. Always stagestruck. Wanted to travel in a trunk. I just couldn't see it. That broke it up. She was sweet, though. Sweet and kind."

"What did it get her? A terrible brute of a husband like Charlie."

"Dad," I said.

"I'll give you that. Charlie has got a terrible temper," said Dad. "Remember when Helen had the lead in our high school graduation play? Pretty as a picture. She wrote some songs for it herself. That was the summer she wrote that song for me."

"Ha," said Mother.

"Don't laugh. It was a good song."

"You never told me about that song."

"It was between Helen and me. Let's see, how *did* it go?"

"Dad," I said.

"You'd better take your daughter out in the back lot," said Mother, "before she collapses. You can sing me that wonderful song later."

"Okay, come on you," said Dad, and I ran him out of the house.

The empty lot was still empty and hot and the glass sparkled green and white and brown all around where the bottles lay.

"Now, where's this Screaming Woman?" laughed Dad.

"We forgot the shovels," I cried.

"We'll get them later, after we hear the soloist," said Dad.

I took him over to the spot. "Listen," I said.

We listened.

"I don't hear anything," said Dad, at last.

"Shh," I said. "Wait."

We listened some more. "Hey, there, Screaming Woman!" I cried.

We heard the sun in the sky. We heard the wind in the trees, real quiet. We heard a bus, far away, running along. We heard a car pass.

That was all.

"Margaret," said Father. "I suggest you go lie down and put a damp cloth on your forehead."

"But she was here," I shouted. "I heard her, screaming and screaming and screaming. See, here's where the ground's been dug up." I called frantically at the earth, "Hey there, you down there!"

"Margaret," said Father. "This is the place where Mr. Kelly dug yesterday, a big hole, to bury his trash and garbage in."

"But during the night," I said, "someone else used Mr. Kelly's burying place to bury a woman. And covered it all over again."

"Well, I'm going back in and take a cool shower," said Dad.

"You won't help me dig?"

"Better not stay out here too long," said Dad. "It's hot."

Dad walked off. I heard the back door slam.

I stamped on the ground. "Darn," I said.

The screaming started again.

She screamed and screamed. Maybe she had been tired and was resting and now she began it all over, just for me.

I stood in the empty lot in the hot sun and I felt like crying. I ran back to the house and banged the door.

"Dad, she's screaming again!"

"Sure, sure," said Dad. "Come on." And he led me to my upstairs bedroom. "Here," he said. He made me lie down and put a cold rag on my head. "Just take it easy."

I began to cry. "Oh, Dad, we can't let her die. She's all buried, like that person in that story by Edgar Allan Poe, and think how awful it is to be screaming and no one paying any attention."

"I forbid you to leave the house," said Dad, worried. "You just lie there the rest of the afternoon." He went out and locked the door. I heard him and Mother talking in the front room. After a while I stopped crying. I got up and tiptoed to the window. My room was upstairs. It seemed high.

I took a sheet off the bed and tied it to the bedpost and let it out the window. Then I climbed out the window and shinnied down until I touched the ground. Then I ran to the garage, quiet, and I got a couple of shovels and I ran to the empty lot. It was hotter than ever. And I started to dig, and all the while I dug, the Screaming Woman screamed...

It was hard work. Shoving in the shovel and lifting the rocks and glass. And I knew I'd be doing it all afternoon and maybe I wouldn't finish in time. What could I do? Run tell other people? But they'd be like Mom and Dad, pay no attention. I just kept digging, all by myself.

About ten minutes later, Dippy Smith came along the path through the empty lot. He's my age and goes to my school.

"Hi, Margaret," he said.

"Hi, Dippy," I gasped.

"What you doing?" he asked.

"Digging."

"For what?"

"I got a Screaming Lady in the ground and I'm digging for her," I said.

"I don't hear no screaming," said Dippy.

"You sit down and wait a while and you'll hear her scream yet. Or better still, help me dig."

"I don't dig unless I hear a scream," he said.

We waited.

"Listen!" I cried. "Did you *hear* it?"

"Hey," said Dippy, with slow appreciation, his eyes gleaming. "That's okay. Do it again."

"Do what again?"

"The scream."

"We got to wait," I said, puzzled.

"Do it again," he insisted, shaking my arm. "Go on." He dug in his pocket for a brown aggie. "Here." He shoved it at me. "I'll give you this marble if you do it again."

A scream came out of the ground.

"Hot dog!" said Dippy. "Teach *me* to do it!" He danced around as if I was a miracle.

"I don't..." I started to say.

"Did you get the *Throw-Your-Voice* book for a dime from that Magic Company in Dallas, Texas?" cried Dippy. "You got one of those tin ventriloquist contraptions in your mouth?"

"Y-yes," I lied, for I wanted him to help. "If you'll help dig, I'll tell you about it later."

"Swell," he said. "Give me a shovel." We both dug together, and from time to time the Woman screamed.

"Boy," said Dippy. "You'd think she was right underfoot. You're wonderful, Maggie." Then he said, "What's her name?"

"Who?"

"The Screaming Woman. You must have a name for her."

"Oh, sure." I thought a moment. "Her name's Wilma Schweiger and she's a rich old woman, ninety-six years old, and she was buried by a man named Spike, who counterfeited ten-dollar bills."

"Yes, *sir*," said Dippy.

"And there's hidden treasure buried with her, and I, I'm a grave robber come to dig her out and get it," I gasped, digging excitedly.

Dippy made his eyes Oriental and mysterious. "Can I be a grave robber, too?" He had a better idea. "Let's pretend it's the Princess Ommanatra, an Egyptian queen, covered with diamonds!"

We kept digging and I thought, oh, we will rescue her, we *will*. If only we keep on!

"Hey, I just got an idea," said Dippy. And he ran off and got a piece of cardboard. He scribbled on it with crayon.

"Keep digging!" I said. "We can't stop!"

"I'm making a sign. See? SLUMBERLAND CEMETERY! We can bury some birds and beetles here, in matchboxes and stuff. I'll go find some butterflies."

"No, Dippy!"

"It's more fun that way. I'll get me a dead cat, too, maybe..."

"Dippy, use your shovel! Please!"

"Aw," said Dippy. "I'm tired. I think I'll go home and take a nap."

"You can't do that."

"Who says so?"

"Dippy, there's something I want to tell you."

"What?"

He gave the shovel a kick.

I whispered in his ear. "There's really a woman buried here."

"Why sure there is," he said. "You said it, Maggie."

"You don't believe me, either."

"Tell me how you throw your voice and I'll keep on digging."

"But I can't tell you, because I'm not doing it," I said. "Look, Dippy. I'll stand way over here and you listen there."

The Screaming Woman screamed again.

"Hey!" said Dippy. "There really *is* a woman here!"

"That's what I tried to say."

"Let's dig!" said Dippy.

We dug for twenty minutes.

"I wonder who she is?"

"I don't know."

"I wonder if it's Mrs. Nelson or Mrs. Turner or Mrs. Bradley. I wonder if she's pretty. Wonder what color her hair is? Wonder if she's thirty or ninety or sixty?"

"Dig!" I said.

The mound grew high.

"Wonder if she'll reward us for digging her up."

"Sure."

"A quarter, do you think?"

"More than that. I bet it's a dollar."

Dippy remembered as he dug. "I read a book once of magic. There was a Hindu with no clothes on who crept down in a grave and slept there sixty days, not eating anything, no malts, no chewing gum or candy, no air, for sixty days." His face fell. "Say, wouldn't it be awful if it was only a radio buried here and us working so hard?"

"A radio's nice, it'd be all ours."

Just then a shadow fell across us.

"Hey, you kids, what you think you're doing?"

We turned. It was Mr. Kelly, the man who owned the empty lot. "Oh, hello, Mr. Kelly," we said.

"Tell you what I want you to do," said Mr. Kelly. "I want you to take those shovels and take that soil and shovel it right back in that hole you been digging. That's what I want you to do."

My heart started beating fast again. I wanted to scream myself.

"But Mr. Kelly, there's a Screaming Woman and..."

"I'm not interested. I don't hear a thing."

"Listen!" I cried.

The scream.

Mr. Kelly listened and shook his head. "Don't hear nothing. Go on now, fill it up and get home with you before I give you my foot!"

We filled the hole all back in again. And all the while we filled it in, Mr. Kelly stood there, arms folded, and the woman screamed, but Mr. Kelly pretended not to hear it.

When we were finished, Mr. Kelly stomped off, saying, "Go on home now. And if I catch you here again..."

I turned to Dippy. "He's the one," I whispered.

"Huh?" said Dippy.

"He *murdered* Mrs. Kelly. He buried her here, after he strangled her, in a box, but she came to. Why, he stood right here and she screamed and he wouldn't pay any attention."

"Hey," said Dippy. "That's right. He stood right here and lied to us."

"There's only one thing to do," I said. "Call the police and have them come arrest Mr. Kelly."

We ran for the corner store telephone.

The police knocked on Mr. Kelly's door five minutes later. Dippy and I were hiding in the bushes, listening.

"Mr. Kelly?" said the police officer.

"Yes, sir, what can I do for you?"

"Is Mrs. Kelly at home?"

"Yes, sir."

"May we see her, sir?"

"Of course. Hey, Anna!"

Mrs. Kelly came to the door and looked out. "Yes, sir?"

"I beg your pardon," apologized the officer. "We had a report that you were buried out in an empty lot, Mrs. Kelly. It sounded like a child made the call, but we had to be certain. Sorry to have troubled you."

"It's those blasted kids," cried Mr. Kelly, angrily. "If I ever catch them, I'll rip 'em limb from limb!"

"Cheezit!" said Dippy, and we both ran.

"What'll we do now?" I said.

"I got to go home," said Dippy. "Boy, we're really in trouble. We'll get a licking for this."

"But what about the Screaming Woman?"

"To heck with her," said Dippy. "We don't dare go near that empty lot again. Old man Kelly'll be waitin' around with his razor strap and lambast heck out'n us. An' I just happened to remember, Maggie. Ain't old man Kelly sort of deaf, hard-of-hearing?"

"Oh, my gosh," I said. "No *wonder* he didn't hear the screams."

"So long," said Dippy. "We sure got in trouble over your darn old ventriloquist voice. I'll be seeing you."

I was left all alone in the world, no one to help me, no one to believe me at all. I just wanted to crawl down in that box with the Screaming Woman and die. The police were after me now, for lying to them, only I didn't know it was a lie, and my father was probably looking for me, too, or would be once he found my bed empty. There was only one last thing to do, and I did it.

I went from house to house, all down the street, near the empty lot. And I rang every bell and when the door opened I said: "I beg your pardon, Mrs. Griswold, but is anyone missing from your house?" or "Hello, Mrs. Pikes, you're looking fine today. Glad to see you *home*." And once I saw that the lady of the house was home I just chatted a while to be polite, and went on down the street.

The hours were rolling along. It was getting late. I kept thinking, oh, there's only so much air in that box with that woman under the earth, and if I don't hurry, she'll suffocate, and I got to rush! So I rang bells and knocked on doors, and it got later, and I was just about to give up and go home, when I knocked on the *last* door, which was the door of Mr. Charlie Nesbitt, who lives next to us. I kept knocking and knocking.

Instead of Mrs. Nesbitt, or Helen as my father calls her, coming to the door, why it was Mr. Nesbitt, Charlie, *himself.*

"Oh," he said. "It's you, Margaret."

"Yes," I said. "Good afternoon."

"What can I do for you, kid?" he said.

"Well, I thought I'd like to see your wife, Mrs. Nesbitt," I said.

"Oh," he said.

"May I?"

"Well, she's gone out to the store," he said.

"I'll wait," I said, and slipped in past him.

"Hey," he said.

I sat down in a chair. "My, it's a hot day," I said, trying to be calm, thinking about the empty lot and air going out of the box, and the screams getting weaker and weaker.

"Say, listen, kid," said Charlie, coming over to me, "I don't think you better wait."

"Oh, sure," I said. "Why not?"

"Well, my wife won't be back," he said.

"Oh?"

"Not today, that is. She's gone to the store, like I said, but, but, she's going on from there to visit her mother. Yeah. She's going to visit her mother, in Schenectady. She'll be back, two or three days, maybe a week."

"That's a shame," I said.

"Why?"

"I wanted to tell her something."

"What?"

"I just wanted to tell her there's a woman buried over in the empty lot, screaming under tons and tons of dirt."

Mr. Nesbitt dropped his cigarette.

"You dropped your cigarette, Mr. Nesbitt," I pointed out, with my shoe.

"Oh, did I? Sure. So I did," he mumbled. "Well, I'll tell Helen when she comes home, your story. She'll be glad to hear it."

"Thanks. It's a real woman."

"How do you know it is?"

"I heard her."

"How, how you know it isn't, well, a *mandrake* root."

"What's that?"

"You know. A mandrake. It's a kind of a plant, kid. They scream.

I know, I read it once. How you know it ain't a mandrake?"

"I never thought of that."

"You better start thinking," he said, lighting another cigarette. He tried to be casual. "Say, kid, you, eh, you *say* anything about this to anyone?"

"Sure, I told lots of people."

Mr. Nesbitt burned his hand on his match.

"Anybody doing anything about it?" he asked.

"No," I said. "They won't believe me."

He smiled. "Of course. Naturally. You're nothing but a kid. Why should they listen to you?"

"I'm going back now and dig her out with a spade," I said.

"Wait."

"I got to go," I said.

"Stick around," he insisted.

"Thanks, but no," I said, frantically.

He took my arm. "Know how to play cards, kid? Black jack?"

"Yes, sir."

He took out a deck of cards from a desk. "We'll have a game."

"I got to go dig."

"Plenty of time for that," he said, quiet. "Anyway, maybe my wife'll be home. Sure. That's it. You wait for her. Wait a while."

"You think she will be?"

"Sure, kid. Say, about that voice; is it very strong?"

"It gets weaker all the time."

Mr. Nesbitt sighed and smiled. "You and your kid games. Here now, let's play that game of black jack, it's more fun than Screaming Women."

"I got to go. It's late."

"Stick around, you got nothing to do."

I knew what he was trying to do. He was trying to keep me in his house until the screaming died down and was gone. He was trying to keep me from helping her. "My wife'll be home in ten minutes," he said. "Sure. Ten minutes. You wait. You sit right there."

We played cards. The clock ticked. The sun went down the sky. It was getting late. The screaming got fainter and fainter in my mind. "I got to go," I said.

"Another game," said Mr. Nesbitt. "Wait another hour, kid. My wife'll come yet. Wait."

In another hour he looked at his watch. "Well, kid, I guess you can go now." And I knew what his plan was. He'd sneak down in the middle of the night and dig up his wife, still alive, and take her somewhere else and bury her, good. "So long, kid. So long." He let me go, because he thought that by now the air must all be gone from the box.

The door shut in my face.

I went back near the empty lot and hid in some bushes. What could I do? Tell my folks? But they hadn't believed me. Call the police on Mr. Charlie Nesbitt? But he said his wife was away visiting. Nobody would believe me!

I watched Mr. Kelly's house. He wasn't in sight. I ran over to the place where the screaming had been and just stood there.

The screaming had stopped. It was so quiet I thought I would never hear a scream again. It was all over. I was too late, I thought.

I bent down and put my ear against the ground.

And then I heard it, way down, way deep, and so faint I could hardly hear it.

The woman wasn't screaming any more. She was singing.

Something about, "I loved you fair, I loved you well."

It was sort of a sad song. Very faint. And sort of broken. All of those hours down under the ground in that box must have sort of made her crazy. All she needed was some air and food and she'd be all right. But she just kept singing, not wanting to scream any more, not caring, just singing.

I listened to the song.

And then I turned and walked straight across the lot and up the steps to my house and I opened the front door.

"Father," I said.

"So there you are!" he cried.

"Father," I said.

"You're going to get a licking," he said.

"She's not screaming any more."

"Don't talk about her!"

"She's singing now," I cried.

"You're not telling the truth!"

"Dad," I said. "She's out there and she'll be dead soon if you don't listen to me. She's out there, singing, and this is what she's singing." I hummed the tune. I sang a few of the words. "I loved you fair, I loved you well…"

Dad's face grew pale. He came and took my arm.

"What did you say?" he said.

I sang it again, "I loved you fair, I loved you well."

"Where did you *hear* that song?" he shouted.

"Out in the empty lot, just now."

"But that's *Helen's* song, the one she wrote, years ago, for *me*!" cried Father. "You *can't* know it. *Nobody* knew it, except Helen and me. I never sang it to anyone, not you or anyone."

"Sure," I said.

"Oh, my God!" cried Father and ran out the door to get a shovel. The last I saw of him he was in the empty lot, digging, and lots of other people with him, digging.

I felt so happy I wanted to cry.

I dialed a number on the phone and when Dippy answered I said, "Hi, Dippy. Everything's fine. Everything's worked out keen. The Screaming Woman isn't screaming any more."

"Swell," said Dippy.

"I'll meet you in the empty lot with a shovel in two minutes," I said.

"Last one there's a monkey! So long!" cried Dippy.

"So long, Dippy!" I said, and ran.

THESE THINGS HAPPEN

I N THE SPRING of the year 1934, Miss Ann Taylor came to teach at the Central School. That was the year she was twenty-four years old and Bob Markham was fourteen. Everyone remembered Ann Taylor. She was the teacher for whom all the children wanted to bring fruit or flowers, and for whom they rolled up the pink and green maps of the world without being asked. She was the woman who always seemed to be passing by on days when the shade was green under the oaks and elms, her face shifting with the bright shadows as she walked until it was all things to all people. She was the fine peaches of summer in the snow of winter, and she was cool milk for cereal on a hot, early summer morning. And those rare few days in the world when the climate was balanced as fine as a maple leaf between winds that blew just right, those were the days like Ann Taylor, and should have been so named on the calendar.

As for Bob Markham, he was the boy who walked alone through town on any October evening with a pack of leaves after him like a horde of Halloween mice. In spring he moved like a slow white fish in the tart waters of the Fox Hill Creek, baking brown with the shine of a chestnut by autumn. Or you might see him on the lawn with the ants crawling over his books as he read through the long afternoons alone, or playing himself a game of chess on his grandmother's porch. You never saw him with any other child.

That spring when Bob was in the ninth grade, Miss Ann Taylor came in through the door of the schoolroom and all the children sat still in their seats while she wrote her name on the board in a nice round lettering.

"My name is Ann Taylor," she said quietly to them, "and I'm your new teacher."

The room seemed suddenly flooded with illumination, as if the roof had moved back. Bob Markham sat with a spit ball hidden in his hand. After a half hour of listening to Miss Taylor, he quietly let the spit ball drop to the floor.

That afternoon after class, he brought in a bucket of water and a rag and began to wash the boards.

"What's this?" She turned from her desk where she had been correcting spelling papers.

"The boards are kind of dirty," said Bob.

"Yes, I know. Are you sure you want to clean them?"

"I suppose I should have asked permission," he said, halting uneasily.

"I think we can pretend you did," she replied, smiling, and at this smile he finished the boards in an amazing burst of speed and pounded the erasers so furiously that the air was full of snow, it seemed, outside the open window.

"Let's see," said Miss Taylor. "You're Bob Markham, aren't you?"

"Yes'm."

"Well, thank you, Bob."

"Could I do them every afternoon?" he asked.

"Don't you think you should let the others try?"

"I'd like to do them," he said. "Every afternoon."

"We'll try it for a while and see," she said.

He lingered.

"I think you'd better run on home," she said finally.

"Good night." He walked slowly and was gone.

The next morning he happened by the place where she took board and room just as she was coming out to walk to school.

"Well, here I am," he said.

"And do you know," she said, "I'm not surprised."

They walked together.

"May I carry your books?" he asked.

"Why, thank you, Bob."

"It's nothing," he said, taking them.

They walked for a few minutes and he did not say a word. She glanced over and slightly down at him and saw how at ease he was and happy he seemed, and she decided to let him break the silence, but he never did. When they reached the edge of the school grounds, he gave the books back to her. "I guess I better leave you here," he said. "The other kids wouldn't understand."

"I'm not sure I do either, Bob."

"Why, we're friends," he said earnestly.

"Bob—" she began.

"Yes'm?"

"Never mind." She walked away.

"I'll be in class," he said.

And he was in class, and he was there after school every afternoon for the next two weeks, never saying a word, quietly washing the boards and cleaning the erasers and rolling up the maps while she worked at her papers. Between them there was that clock silence of four o'clock, the silence of the sun going down, the silence with the catlike sound of erasers patted together, the rustle and turn of papers and the scratch of a pen, and perhaps the buzz of a fly banging with a tiny high anger against the tallest window in the room. Sometimes the silence would go on this way until almost five, when Miss Taylor would find Bob Markham in the last seat of the room, sitting and looking at her silently.

"Well, it's time to go home," Miss Taylor would say, getting up.

"Yes'm."

And he would run to fetch her hat and coat. He would also lock the schoolroom door for her unless the janitor was coming in later. Then they would walk out of the school and across the empty yard. They talked of all sorts of things.

"And what are you going to be, Bob, when you grow up?"

"A writer," he said.

"Oh, that's a big ambition. It takes a lot of work."

"I know, but I'm going to try," he said. "I've read a lot."

"Bob, haven't you anything to do after school? I mean, I hate to see you indoors so much, washing the boards."

"I like it," he said. "I never do what I don't like."

"Nevertheless—"

"No. I've got to do that," he said. He thought for a while and said, "Do me a favor, Miss Taylor?"

"It all depends."

"I walk every Saturday from out around Buetrick Street along the creek to Lake Michigan. There's a lot of butterflies and crayfish and birds. Maybe you'd like to walk too."

"Thank you," she said.

"Then you'll come?"

"I'm afraid I'm going to be busy."

He started to ask doing what, but stopped.

"I take along sandwiches," he said. "Ham and pickle ones. And orange pop. I get down to the lake about noon and walk back about three. I wish you'd come. Do you collect butterflies? I have a big collection. We could start one for you."

"Thanks, Bob, but no. Perhaps some other time."

He looked at her and said, "I shouldn't have asked you, should I?"

"You have every right to ask anything you want to," she said.

A FEW DAYS later she found an old copy of *Great Expectations* which she didn't want, and gave it to Bob. He stayed up that night and read it through and talked about it the next morning. Each day now he met her just beyond sight of her boarding-house, and many days she would start to say, "Bob—" and tell him not to come to meet her any more, but she never finished saying it.

She found a butterfly on her desk on Friday morning. She almost waved it away before she found that it was dead and had been placed there while she was out of the room. She glanced at Bob over the heads of her other students, but he was looking at his book—not reading, just looking at it.

It was about this time that she found it impossible to call on Bob to recite in class. Her pencil would hover over his name and then she would call the next person up or down the list. Nor would she look at him while they were walking to or from school. But on several late afternoons as he moved his arm high on the blackboard, sponging away the arithmetic symbols, she found herself glancing over at him for seconds at a time.

And then one Saturday morning when he was standing in the middle of the creek with his overalls rolled up to his knees, he looked up and there on the edge of the running stream was Miss Ann Taylor.

"Well, here I am," she said, laughing.

"And do you know," he said, "I'm not surprised."

"Show me the crayfish and the butterflies," she said.

They walked down to the lake and sat on the sand with a warm wind blowing softly about them. He sat a few yards back from her while they ate the ham and pickle sandwiches and drank the orange pop solemnly.

"Gee, this is swell," he said. "This is the swellest time ever in my life."

"I didn't think I would ever come on a picnic like this," she said.

"With some kid," he said.

"I'm comfortable, however," she said.

"That's good news."

They said little else during the afternoon.

"This is all wrong," he said later. "And I can't figure why it should be. Just walking along and catching old butterflies and crayfish and eating sandwiches. But Mom and Dad'd rib the heck out of me if they knew, and the kids would too. And the other teachers, I suppose, would laugh at you, wouldn't they?"

"I'm afraid so."

"I guess we better not do any more butterfly-catching, then."

"I don't exactly understand how I came here at all," she said.

And the day was over.

T HAT WAS about all there was to the meeting of Ann Taylor
and Bob Markham. Two or three monarch butterflies, a copy
of Dickens, a dozen crayfish, four sandwiches, and two bottles
of orange pop. The next Monday, though he waited a long time,
Bob did not see Miss Taylor come out to walk to school. He
discovered later she had left earlier and was already there. Also,
Monday afternoon she left early and another teacher finished her
last class. He walked by her boarding-house and did not see her
anywhere, but he was afraid to ring the bell and inquire.

On Tuesday night after school they both were in the silent room
again, he sponging the board contentedly as if this time might go on
forever, and she seated working on her papers as if she, too, would be
in this room and this particular peace and happiness forever, when
suddenly the court-house clock struck. It was a block away and its
great bronze boom shuddered one's body, making you seem older
by the minute. Stunned by that clock, you could not but sense the
crashing flow of time, and as the clock said five o'clock Miss Taylor
looked up at it for a long time. Then she put down her pen.

"Bob," she said.

He turned, startled. Neither of them had spoken in the peaceful
hour before.

"Will you come here?" she asked.

He put down the sponge slowly.

"Yes," he said.

"Bob, I want you to sit down."

"Yes'm."

She looked at him intently for a moment until he looked away.
"Bob, I wonder if you know what I'm going to talk to you about?
Do you know?"

"Yes."

"Maybe you should tell me first."

"About us." he said at last.

"How old are you, Bob?"

"Going on fifteen."

"You're fourteen years old."

He winced. "Yes'm."

"And do you know how old I am?"

"Yes'm. I heard. Twenty-four."

"Twenty-four."

"I'll be twenty-four in ten years," he said.

"But unfortunately you're not twenty-four now."

"No, but sometimes I feel twenty-four."

"Yes, and sometimes you act it."

"Do I, really?"

"Now sit still there; we've a lot to discuss. It's very important that we understand what is happening, isn't it?"

"Yes, I guess so."

FIRST, LET'S admit we are the greatest and best friends in the world. Let's admit that I have never had a student like you, nor have I had as much affection for any boy I've ever known. And let me speak for you, you've found me to be the nicest of all the teachers you've ever known."

"Oh, more than that," he said.

"Perhaps more than that, but there are facts to be faced and an entire way of life to be examined, and a town and its people and you and I to be considered. I've thought this over for a good many days, Bob. Don't think I've been unaware of my own feelings in the matter. Under some circumstances our friendship would be odd indeed. But then you are no ordinary boy. I know myself pretty well, I think, and I know that I'm not sick, either mentally or physically, and that what I feel is a true regard for your character. But that is not what we consider in this world, Bob, except in a man of a certain age. I don't know if I'm saying this right."

"It's all right," he said. "It's just that if I were ten years older, and about fifteen inches taller it'd make all the difference. And that's silly, to go by how tall a person is."

"I know it seems foolish," she said, "when you feel very grown-up and right and have nothing to be ashamed of. You have nothing at all to be ashamed of, Bob—remember that. You have been very honest and good, and I hope that I have been too."

"You have," he said.

"Maybe someday people will judge the oldness of a person's mind accurately enough to say, 'This is a man, though his body is only fourteen. By some miracle of circumstance and fortune, this is a man, with a man's recognition of responsibility and position and duty.' But until that day, Bob, I'm afraid we're going to have to go by ages and heights in the ordinary way."

"I don't like that," he said.

"Perhaps I don't like it either, but do you want to end up far unhappier than you are now? Do you want both of us to be unhappy? Which we would certainly be. There really is no way to do anything about us; it is strange even to try to talk about us."

"Yes'm."

"But at least we know all about us and that we have been right and fair and good, and that there is nothing wrong with our knowing each other. But we both understand how impossible it is, don't we?"

"Yes—but I can't help it."

"We must decide what to do about it," she said. "Now only you and I know about this. Later others might know. I can transfer from this school to another one—"

"No!"

"Or I can have you transferred."

"You don't have to do that," he said.

"Why?"

"We're moving. My folks and I, we're going to live in Madison. We're leaving next week."

"It has nothing to do with all this, has it?"

"No, no, everything's all right. It's just my father has a new job there. It's only fifty miles away. I can see you, can't I, when I come to town?"

"Do you think that would be a good idea?"

"No, I guess not."

They sat a while in the silent school room.

"How did all of this happen?" he said helplessly.

"I don't know," she said. "Nobody ever knows. They haven't known for thousand of years, and I don't think they ever will. People either like each other or don't, and sometimes two people like each other who shouldn't. I can't explain myself, and certainly you can't explain you."

"I guess I'd better get home," he said.

"You're not mad at me, are you?"

"Oh, gosh no, I could never be mad at you."

"There's one more thing. I want you to remember—there are compensations in life. There always are, or we wouldn't go on living. You don't feel happy now; neither do I. But something will happen to fix that. Do you believe that?"

"I'd like to."

"Well, it's true."

"If only—" he said.

"What?"

"If only you'd wait for me," he blurted.

"Ten years?"

"I'd be twenty-four then."

"But I'd be thirty-four and another person entirely, perhaps. No, I don't think it can be done."

"Wouldn't you like it to be done?" he cried.

"Yes," she said quietly. "It's silly and it wouldn't work, but I would like it very much."

He sat there for a long time. "I'll never forget you," he said.

"It's nice for you to say that, even though it can't be true, because life isn't that way. You'll forget."

"I'll never forget. I'll find a way of never forgetting you," he said.

She got up and went to the board.

"I'll help you," he said.

"No, no," she said hastily. "You can go on now, and no more tending to the boards after school. I'll assign Helen Stevens to do it."

He left the room. Looking back, outside, he saw Miss Ann Taylor for the last time. She was standing at the board, slowly erasing it.

H E MOVED away from town the next week and he was gone for sixteen years. He never got down to Green Bluff again until he was thirty and married. And then one spring he and his wife were driving through on their way to Chicago and stopped off there.

Alone, he took a walk around town and finally asked about Miss Ann Taylor. No one remembered at first and then one of them did.

"Oh, yes, the pretty teacher. She died not long after you left."

Had she ever married? No, come to think of it, she never had.

He walked out to the cemetery in the afternoon and found her stone, which said, "Ann Taylor, born 1910, died 1936." And he thought, Twenty-six years old. Why, I'm four years older than you are now, Miss Taylor.

Later in the day the people in the town saw Bob Markham's wife strolling to meet him and they all turned to watch her pass, for her face shifted with bright shadows as she walked. She was the fine peaches of summer in the snow of winter, and she was cool milk for cereal on a hot early summer morning. And this was one of those rare few days in time when the climate was balanced like a maple leaf between winds that blow just right, one of those days that should have been named, everyone agreed, after Bob Markham's wife.

AT MIDNIGHT, IN THE MONTH OF JUNE

H E HAD BEEN waiting a long, long time in the summer
night, as the darkness pressed warmer to the earth and the
stars turned slowly over the sky. He sat in total darkness,
his hands lying easily on the arms of the Morris chair.
He heard the town clock strike 9 and 10 and 11, and then at
last 12. The breeze from an open back window flowed through
the midnight house in an unlit stream, that touched him like a
dark rock where he sat silently watching the front door—silently
watching.

At midnight, in the month of June....

The cool night poem by Mr. Edgar Allan Poe slid over his
mind like the waters of a shadowed creek.

> *The lady sleeps! Oh, may her sleep,*
> *Which is enduring, so be deep!*

He moved down the black shapeless halls of the house, stepped
out of the back window, feeling the town locked away in bed, in
dream, in night. He saw the shining snake of garden hose coiled
resiliently in the grass. He turned on the water. Standing alone,
watering the flower bed, he imagined himself a conductor leading
an orchestra that only night-strolling dogs might hear, passing on

their way to nowhere with strange white smiles. Very carefully he planted both feet and his tall weight into the mud beneath the window, making deep, well-outlined prints. He stepped inside again and walked, leaving mud, down the absolutely unseen hall, his hands seeing for him.

Through the front-porch window he made out the faint outline of a lemonade glass, one-third full, sitting on the porch rail where *she* had left it. He trembled quietly.

Now, he could feel her coming home. He could feel her moving across town, far away, in the summer night. He shut his eyes and put his mind out to find her; and felt her moving along in the dark; he knew just where she stepped down from a curb and crossed a street, and up on a curb and tack-tacking, tack-tacking along under the June elms and the last of the lilacs, with a friend. Walking the empty desert of night, he *was* she. He felt a purse in his hands. He felt long hair prickle his neck, and his mouth turn greasy with lipstick. Sitting still, he was walking, walking, walking on home after midnight.

"Good night!"

He heard but did not hear the voices, and she was coming nearer, and now she was only a mile away and now only a matter of a thousand yards, and now she was sinking, like a beautiful white lantern on an invisible wire, down into the cricket and frog and water-sounding ravine. And he knew the texture of the wooden ravine stairs as if, a boy, he was rushing down them, feeling the rough grain and the dust and the leftover heat of the day...

He put his hands out on the air, open. The thumbs of his hands touched, and then the fingers, so that his hands made a circle, enclosing emptiness, there before him. Then, very slowly, he squeezed his hands tighter and tighter together, his mouth open, his eyes shut.

He stopped squeezing and put his hands, trembling, back on the arms of the chair. He kept his eyes shut.

Long ago, he had climbed, one night, to the top of the courthouse tower fire-escape, and looked out at the silver town, at the town of the moon, and the town of summer. And he had seen all the dark houses with two things in them, people and sleep, the two elements joined in bed and all their tiredness and terror breathed upon the still air, siphoned back quietly, and breathed out again, until that element was purified, the problems and hatreds and horrors of the previous day exorcised long before morning and done away with forever.

He had been enchanted with the hour, and the town, and he had felt very powerful, like the magic man with the marionettes who strung destinies across a stage on spider-threads. On the very top of the courthouse tower he could see the least flicker of leaf turning in the moonlight five miles away; the last light, like a pink pumpkin eye, wink out. The town did not escape his eye—it could do nothing without his knowing its every tremble and gesture.

And so it was tonight. He felt himself a tower with the clock in it pounding slow and announcing hours in a great bronze tone, and gazing upon a town where a woman, hurried or slowed by fitful gusts and breezes of now terror and now self-confidence, took the chalk-white midnight sidewalks home, fording solid avenues of tar and stone, drifting among fresh cut lawns, and now running, running down the steps, through the ravine, up, up the . hill, up the hill!

He heard her footsteps before he really heard them. He heard her gasping before there was a gasping. He fixed his gaze to the lemonade glass outside, on the banister. Then the real sound, the real running, the gasping, echoed wildly outside. He sat up. The footsteps raced across the street, the sidewalk, in a panic. There was a babble, a clumsy stumble up the porch steps, a key racketing the door, a voice yelling in a whisper, praying to itself, "Oh, God, dear God!" Whisper! Whisper! And the woman crashing in the door, slamming it, bolting it, talking, whispering, talking to herself in the dark room.

He felt, rather than saw, her hands move toward the light switch. He cleared his throat.

SHE STOOD against the door in the dark. If moonlight could have struck in upon her, she would have shimmered like a small pool of water on a windy night. He felt the fine sapphire jewels come out upon her face, and her face all glittering with brine.

"Lavinia," he whispered.

Her arms were raised across the door like a crucifix. He heard her mouth open and her lungs push a warmness upon the air. She was a beautiful dim white moth; with the sharp needle point of terror he had her pinned against the wooden door. He could walk all around the specimen if he wished, and look at her, look at her.

"Lavinia," he whispered.

He heard her heart beating. She did not move.

"It's me," he whispered.

"Who?" she said, so faint it was a small pulse-beat in her throat.

"I won't tell you," he whispered. He stood perfectly straight in the center of the room. God, but he felt *tall!* Tall and dark and very beautiful to himself, and the way his hands were out before him was as if he might play a piano at any moment, a lovely melody, a waltzing tune. The hands were wet, they felt as if he had dipped them into a bed of mint and cool menthol.

"If I told you who I am, you might not be afraid," he whispered. "I want you to be afraid. Are you afraid?"

She said nothing. She breathed out and in, out and in, a small bellows which, pumped steadily, blew upon her fear and kept it going, kept it alight.

"Why did you go to the show tonight?" he whispered. "*Why* did you go to the show?"

No answer.

He took a step forward, heard her breath take itself, like a sword hissing in its sheath.

"Why did you come back through the ravine alone?" he whispered. "You *did* come back alone, didn't you? Did you think you'd meet me in the middle of the bridge? Why did you go to the show tonight? Why did you come back through the ravine, alone?"

"I—" she gasped.

"You," he whispered.

"No—" she cried, in a whisper.

"Lavinia," he said. He took another step.

"Please," she said.

"Open the door. Get out. And run," he whispered.

She did not move.

"Lavinia, open the door."

She began to whimper in her throat.

"Run," he said.

In moving, he felt something touch his knee. He pushed, something tilted in space and fell over, a table, a basket, and a half-dozen unseen balls of yarn tumbled like cats in the dark, rolling softly. In the one moonlit space on the floor beneath the window, like a metal sign pointing, lay the sewing shears. They were winter ice in his hand. He held them out to her suddenly, through the still air.

"Here," he whispered.

He touched them to her hand. She snatched her hand back.

"Here," he urged.

"Take this," he said, after a pause.

He opened her fingers that were already dead and cold to the touch, and stiff and strange to manage, and he pressed the scissors into them. "Now," he said.

He looked out at the moonlit sky for a long moment, and when he glanced back it was some time before he could see her in the dark.

"I waited," he said. "But that's the way it's always been. I waited for the others, too. But they all came looking for me, finally. It was that easy. Five lovely ladies in the last two years. I waited for them in the ravine, in the country, by the lake, everywhere I waited, and they came out to find me, and found me. It was always nice, the next day, reading the newspapers. And you went looking tonight,

I know, or you wouldn't have come back alone through the ravine. Did you scare yourself there, and run? Did you think I was down there waiting for you? You should have *heard* yourself running up the walk! Through the door! And *locking* it! You thought you were safe inside, home at last, safe, safe, safe, didn't you?"

She held the scissors in one dead hand, and she began to cry. He saw the merest gleam, like water upon the wall of a dim cave. He heard the sounds she made.

"No," he whispered. "You have the scissors. Don't cry."

She cried. She did not move at all. She stood there, shivering, her head back against the door, beginning to slide down the length of the door toward the floor.

"Don't cry," he whispered.

"I don't like to hear you cry," he said. "I can't stand to hear that."

He held his hands out and moved them through the air until one of them touched her cheek. He felt the wetness of that cheek, he felt her warm breath touch his palm like a summer moth. Then he said only one more thing:

"Lavinia," he said, gently, "Lavinia."

H OW CLEARLY he remembered the old nights in the old times, in the times when he was a boy and them all running, and running, and hiding and hiding, and playing hide-and-seek. In the first spring nights and in the warm summer nights and in the late summer evenings and in those first sharp autumn nights when doors were shutting early and porches were empty except for blowing leaves. The game of hide-and-seek went on as long as there was sun to see by, or the rising snow-crusted moon. Their feet upon the green lawns were like the scattered throwing of soft peaches and crabapples, and the counting of the Seeker with his arms cradling his buried head, chanting to the night: five, ten, fifteen, twenty, twenty-five, thirty, thirty-five, forty, forty-five, fifty...And the sound of thrown apples fading, the children all safely closeted in tree or bush-shade, under the latticed porches with the clever dogs minding not to wag their tails and give their secret away. And the counting done: eighty-five, ninety, ninety-five, a hundred!

Ready or not, here I come!

And the Seeker running out through the town wilderness to find the Hiders, and the Hiders keeping their secret laughter in their mouths, like precious June strawberries, with the help of clasped hands. And the Seeker seeking after the smallest heartbeat in the high elm tree or the glint of a dog's eye in a bush, or a small water sound of laughter which could not help but burst out as the Seeker ran right on by and did not see the shadow within the shadow...

He moved into the bathroom of the quiet house, thinking all this, enjoying the clear rush, the tumultuous gushing of memories like a water falling of the mind over a steep precipice, falling and falling toward the bottom of his head.

God, how secret and tall they had felt, hidden away. God, how the shadows mothered and kept them, sheathed in their own triumph. Glowing with perspiration how they crouched like idols and thought they might hide *forever!* While the silly Seeker went pelting by on his way to failure and inevitable frustration.

Sometimes the Seeker stopped right *at* your tree and peered up at you crouched there in your invisible warm wings, in your great colorless windowpane bat wings, and said "I see you there!" But you said nothing. "You're *up* there all right." But you said nothing. "Come on *down!*" But not a word, only a victorious Cheshire smile. And doubt coming over the Seeker below. "It is *you*, isn't it?" The backing off and away, "Aw, I *know* you're up there!" No answer. Only the tree sitting in the night and shaking quietly, leaf upon leaf. And the Seeker, afraid of the dark within darkness, loping away to seek easier game, something to be named and certain of. "All right for *you!*"

He washed his hands in the bathroom, and thought, Why am I washing my hands?

And then the grains of time sucked back up the flue of the hour-glass again and it was another year...

He remembered that sometimes when he played hide-and-seek they did not find him at all; he would not let them find him. He said not a word, he stayed so long in the apple tree that he was a white-fleshed apple; he lingered so long in the chestnut tree that he had the hardness and the brown brightness of the autumn nut. And God, how powerful to be undiscovered, how immense it made you, until your arms were branching, growing out in all directions, pulled by the stars and the tidal moon until your secretness enclosed the town and mothered it with your compassion and tolerance. You could do anything in the shadows, anything. If you chose to do it, you could do it. How powerful to sit above the sidewalk and see people pass under, never aware you were there and watching, and might put out an arm to brush their noses with the five-legged spider of your hand and brush their thinking minds with terror.

He finished washing his hands and wiped them on a towel.

But there was always an end to the game. When the Seeker had found all the other Hiders and these Hiders in turn were Seekers and they were all spreading out, calling your name, looking for you, how much more powerful and important *that* made you.

"Hey, hey! Where *are* you! Come in, the game's *over!*"

But you not moving or coming in. Even when they all collected under your tree and saw, or thought they saw you there at the very top, and called up at you. "Oh, come down! Stop fooling! Hey! We see you. We know you're there!"

Not answering even, then—not until the final, the fatal thing happened. Far off, a block away, a silver whistle screaming, and the voice of your mother calling your name, and the whistle again. "Nine o'clock!" her voice wailed. "Nine o'clock! Home!"

But you waited until all the children were gone. Then, very carefully unfolding yourself and your warmth and secretness, and keeping out of the lantern light at corners, you ran home alone, alone in the darkness and shadow, hardly breathing, keeping the sound of your heart quiet and in yourself, so if people heard anything at all they might think it was only the wind blowing a dry leaf by in the night. And your mother standing there, with the screen door wide…

He finished wiping his hands on the towel. He stood a moment thinking of how it had been the last two years here in town. The old game going on, by himself, playing it alone, the children gone, grown into settled middle-age, but now, as before, himself the final and last and only Hider, and the whole town seeking and seeing nothing and going on home to lock their doors.

But tonight, out of a time long past, and on many nights now, he had heard that old sound, the sound of the silver whistle, blowing and blowing. It was certainly not a night bird singing, for he knew each sound so well. But the whistle kept calling and calling and a voice said, *Home* and *Nine o'clock*, even though it was now long after midnight. He listened. There was the silver whistle. Even though his mother had died many years ago, after having put his father in an early grave with her temper and her tongue. "Do this, do that, do this, do that, do this, do that, do this, do that…" A phonograph record, broken, playing the same cracked tune again, again, again, her voice, her cadence, around, around, around, around, repeat, repeat, repeat.

And the clear silver whistle blowing and the game of hide-and-seek over. No more of walking in the town and standing behind trees and bushes and smiling a smile that burned through the thickest foliage. An automatic thing was happening. His feet were walking and his hands were doing and he knew everything that must be done now.

His hands did not belong to him.

He tore a button off his coat and let it drop into the deep dark well of the room. It never seemed to hit bottom. It floated down. He waited.

It seemed never to stop rolling. Finally, it stopped.

His hands did not belong to him.

He took his pipe and flung that into the depths of the room. Without waiting for it to strike emptiness, he walked quietly back through the kitchen and peered outside the open, blowing, white-curtained window at the footprints he had made there. He was the Seeker, seeking now, instead of the Hider hiding. He was the quiet searcher finding and sifting and putting away clues, and those footprints were now as alien to him as something from a prehistoric age. They had been made a million years ago by some other man on some other business; they were no part of him at all. He marvelled at their precision and deepness and form in the moonlight. He put his hand down almost to touch them, like a great and beautiful archeological discovery! Then he was gone, back through the rooms, ripping a piece of material from his pants-cuff and blowing it off his open palm like a moth.

His hands were not his hands any more, or his body his body.

He opened the front door and went out and sat for a moment on the porch rail. He picked up the lemonade glass and drank what was left, made warm by an evening's waiting, and pressed his fingers tight to the glass, tight, tight, very tight. Then he put the glass down on the railing.

The silver whistle!

Yes, he thought. Coming, coming.

The silver whistle!

Yes, he thought. Nine o'clock. Home, home. Nine o'clock. Studies and milk and graham crackers and white cool bed, home, home; nine o'clock and the silver whistle.

He was off the porch in an instant, running softly, lightly, with hardly a breath or a heartbeat, as one barefooted runs, as one all leaf and green June grass and night can run, all shadow, forever running, away from the silent house and across the street, and down into the ravine...

H E PUSHED the door wide and stepped into the owl diner, this long railroad car that, removed from its track, had been put to a solitary and unmoving destiny in the center of town. The place was empty. At the far end of the counter, the counterman glanced up as the door shut and the customer walked along the line of empty swivel seats. The counterman took the toothpick from his mouth.

"Tom Dillon, you old so-and-so! What *you* doing up this time of night, Tom?"

Tom Dillon ordered without the menu. While the food was being prepared, he dropped a nickel in the wall-phone, got his number, and spoke quietly for a time. He hung up, came back, and sat, listening. Sixty seconds later, both he and counterman heard the police siren wail by at 50 miles an hour. "Well—*hell!*" said the counterman. "Go get 'em, boys!"

He set out a tall glass of milk and a plate of six fresh graham crackers.

Tom Dillon sat there for a long while, looking secretly down at his ripped pants-cuff and muddied shoes. The light in the diner was raw and bright, and he felt like he was on a stage. He held the tall cool glass of milk in his hand, sipping it, eyes shut, chewing the good texture of the graham crackers, feeling it all through his mouth, coating his tongue.

"Would or would you not." he asked, quietly, "call this a hearty meal?"

"I'd call that very hearty indeed," said the counterman, smiling.

Tom Dillon chewed another graham cracker with great concentration, feeling all of it in his mouth. It's just a matter of time, he thought, waiting.

"More milk?"

"Yes," said Tom.

And he watched with steady interest, with the purest and most alert concentration in all of his life, as the white carton tilted and gleamed, and the snowy milk poured out, cool and quiet, like the sound of a running spring at night, and filled the glass up all the way, to the very brim, to the very brim, and over…

A WALK IN SUMMER

THE ROOM WAS like the bottom of a cool well all night and she lay in it like a white stone in a well, enjoying it, floating in the dark yet clear element of half-dreams and half-wakening. She felt the breath move in small jets from her nostrils and she felt the immense sweep of her eyelids shutting and opening again and again. And at last she felt the fever brought into her room by the presence of the sun beyond the hills.

"Morning," she thought. "It might be a special day. Anything might happen. And I hope it does."

The air moved the white curtains like a summer breath.

"Vinia…?"

A voice was calling. But it couldn't be a voice. Yet—Vinia raised herself—there it was again.

"Vinia…?"

She slipped from bed and ran to the window of her high second story bedroom.

There on the fresh lawn below, calling up to her in the early hour, stood James Conway, no older than herself, sixteen, very seriously smiling, waving his hand now as her head appeared.

"Jim, what're you doing here?" she said.

"I've been up an hour already," he replied. "I'm going for a walk, starting early, all day. Want to come along?"

"Oh, but I couldn't...My folks won't be back 'till late tonight, I'm alone, I'm supposed to stay..."

She saw the green hills beyond the town and the roads leading out into summer, leading out into August and rivers and places beyond this town and this house and this room and this particular moment.

"I can't go..." she said, faintly.

"I can't hear you!" he protested, mildly, smiling up at her under a shielding hand.

"Why did you ask me to walk with you and not someone else?"

He considered this a moment. "I don't know," he admitted. He thought it over again, and gave her his most pleasant and agreeable look. "Because, that's all, just because."

"I'll be down," she said.

"Hey!" he said.

But the window was empty.

THEY STOOD in the center of the perfect, jewelled lawn, over which one set of prints, hers, had run leaving marks, and another, his, had walked in great slow strides, to meet them. The town was silent as a stopped clock. All the shades were still down.

"My gosh," said Vinia, "it's early. It's crazy-early. I've never been up this early and out this early in years. Listen to everyone sleeping."

They listened to the trees and the whiteness of the house in this early whispering hour, the hour when mice went back to sleep and flowers began untightening their bright fists.

"Which way do we go?"

"Pick a direction."

Vinia closed her eyes, whirled, and pointed blindly. "Which way am I pointing?"

"North."

She opened her eyes. "Let's go north out of town then. I don't suppose we should."

"Why?"

And they walked out of town as the sun rose above the hills and the grass burned greener on the lawns.

THERE WAS a smell of hot chalk highway, of dust and sky and waters flowing in a creek the color of grapes. The sun was a new lemon. The forest lay ahead with shadows stirring like a million birds under each tree, each bird a leaf-darkness trembling. At noon, Vinia and James Conway had crossed vast meadows that sounded brisk and starched underfoot. The day had grown warm, as an iced glass of tea grows warm, the frost burning off, left in the sun.

They picked a handful of grapes from a wild barbed-wire vine. Holding them up to the sun you could see the clear grape thoughts suspended in the dark amber fluid, the little hot seeds of contemplation stored from many afternoons of solitude and plant philosophy. The grapes tasted of fresh clear water and something that they had saved from the morning dews and the evening rains. They were the warmed over flesh of April ready now, in August, to pass on their simple gain to any passing stranger. And the lesson was this: sit in the sun, head down, within a prickly vine, in flickery light or open light, and the world will come to you. The sky will come in its time, bringing rain, and the earth will rise through you, from beneath, and make you rich and make you full.

"Have a grape," said James Conway. "Have *two*."

They munched their wet, full mouths.

They sat on the edge of a brook and took off their shoes and let the water cut their feet off to the ankles with an exquisite cold razor.

"My feet are gone!" thought Vinia. But when she looked, there they were, underwater, living comfortably apart from her, completely acclimated to an amphibious existence.

They ate egg sandwiches Jim had brought with him in a paper sack.

"Vinia," said Jim, looking at his sandwich before he bit it. "Would you mind if I kissed you?"

"I don't know," she said, after a moment. "I hadn't thought."

"Will you think it over?" he asked.

"Did we come on this picnic just so you could kiss me?" she asked, suddenly.

"Oh, don't get me wrong! It's been a swell day! I don't want to spoil it. But if you should decide later, that it's all right for me to kiss you, would you tell me?"

"I'll tell you," she said, starting on her second sandwich, "if I ever decide."

THE RAIN came as a cool surprise.

It smelled of soda water and limes and oranges and the cleanest freshest river in the world, made of snow-water, falling from the high, parched sky.

First there had been a motion, as of veils, in the sky. The clouds had enveloped each other softly. A faint breeze had lifted Vinia's hair, sighing and evaporating the moisture from her upper lip, and then, as she and Jim began to run, the raindrops fell down all about without touching them and then at last began to touch them, coolly, as they leaped green-moss logs and darted among vast trees into the deepest, muskiest cavern of the forest. The forest sprang up in wet murmurs overhead, every leaf ringing and painted fresh with water.

"This way!" cried Jim.

And they reached a hollow tree so vast that they could squeeze in and be warmly cozy from the rain. They stood together, arms about each other, the first coldness from the rain making them shiver, raindrops on their noses and cheeks, laughing.

"Hey!" He gave her brow a lick. "Drinking water!"

"Jim!"

They listened to the rain, the soft envelopment of the world in the velvet clearness of falling water, the whispers in deep grass, evoking odors of old wet wood and leaves that had lain a hundred years, mouldering and sweet.

Then they heard another sound. Above and inside the hollow

warm darkness of the tree was a constant humming, like someone in a kitchen, far away, baking and crusting pies, contentedly,
dipping in sweet sugars and snowing in baking powders, someone
in a warm dim summer-rainy kitchen making a vast supply of
food, happy at it, humming between lips over it.

"Bees, Jim, up there! Bees!"

"Sh!"

Up the channel of moist warm hollow they saw little yellow
flickers. Now the last bees, wettened, were hurrying home from
whatever pasture or meadow or field they had covered, dipping
by Vinia and Jim, vanishing up the warm flue of summer into
hollow dark.

"They won't bother us. Just stand still."

Jim tightened his arms, Vinia tightened hers. She could smell
his breath with the wild tart grapes still on it. And the harder the
rain drummed on the tree, the tighter they held, laughing, at last
quietly letting their laughter drain away into the sound of the bees
home from the far fields. And for a moment, Vinia thought that
she and Jim might be caught by a sudden drop of great masses of
honey from above, sealing them into this tree forever, enchanted,
in amber, to be seen by anyone in the next thousand years who
strolled by, while the weather of all ages rained and thundered
and turned green outside the tree.

It was so warm, so safe, so protected here, the world did not
exist, there was raining silence, in the sunless, forested day.

"Vinia," whispered Jim, after awhile. "May I now?"

His face was very large, near her, larger than any face she had
ever seen.

"Yes," she said.

He kissed her.

The rain poured hard on the tree for a full minute while
everything was cold outside and everything was tree-warmth and
hidden away inside.

It was a very sweet kiss. It was very friendly and comfortably
warm and it tasted like apricots and fresh apples and as water

tastes when you rise at night and walk into a dark warm summer kitchen and drink from a cool tin cup. She had never imagined that a kiss could be so sweet and immensely tender and careful of her. He held her not as he had held her a moment before, hard, to protect her from the green rain weather, but he held her now as if she were a porcelain clock, very carefully and with consideration. His eyes were closed and the lashes were glistening dark; she saw this in the instant she opened her eyes and closed them again.

The rain stopped.

It was a moment before the new silence shocked them into an awareness of the climate beyond their world. Now there was nothing but the suspension of water in all the intricate branches of the forest. Clouds moved away to show the blue sky in great quilted patches.

They looked out at the change with some dismay. They waited for the rain to come back, to keep them, by necessity, in this hollow tree for another minute or an hour. But the sun appeared, shining through upon everything, making the scene quite commonplace again.

They stepped from the hollow tree slowly and stood, with their hands out, balancing, finding their way, it seemed, in these woods where the water was drying fast on every limb and leaf.

"I think we'd better start walking," said Vinia. "That way."

They walked off into the summer afternoon.

THEY CROSSED the town-limits at sunset and walked, hand in hand in the last glowing of the summer day. They had talked very little the rest of the afternoon, and now as they turned down one street after another, they looked at the passing sidewalk under their feet.

"Vinia," he said at last. "Do you think this is the beginning of something?"

"Oh, gosh, Jim, I don't know."

"Do you think maybe we're in love?"

"Oh, I don't know that either!"

They passed down the ravine and over the bridge and up the other side to her street.

"Do you think we'll ever be married?"

"It's too early to tell, isn't it?" she said.

"I guess you're right." He bit his lip. "Will we go walking again soon?"

"I don't know. I don't know. Let's wait and see, Jim."

The house was dark, her parents not home yet. They stood on her porch and she shook his hand gravely.

"Thanks, Jim, for a really fine day," she said.

"You're welcome," he said.

They stood there.

Then he turned and walked down the steps and across the dark lawn. At the far edge of lawn he stopped in the shadows and said, "Good night."

He was almost out of sight, running, when she, in turn, said good night.

I N THE middle of the night, a sound wakened her.

She half sat up in bed, trying to hear it again. The folks were home, everything was locked and secure, but it hadn't been them. No, this was a special sound. And, lying there, looking out at the summer night that had, not long ago, been a summer day, she heard the sound again, and it was a sound of hollowing warmth and moist bark and empty, tunnelled tree, and rain outside but comfortable dryness and secretness inside, and it was the sound of bees come home from distant fields, moving upward in the flue of summer into wonderful darkness.

And this sound, she realized, putting her hand up in the summer night room to touch it, was coming from her sleepy, half-smiling mouth.

And it was this sound, eventually, which sang her to sleep.

AUTUMN AFTERNOON

"I T'S A VERY sad time of year to be cleaning out the attic," said Grandma. "I don't like autumn, sometimes. Don't like the way the trees get empty. And the sky always looks like the sun had bleached it out." She stood hesitantly at the bottom of the attic stairs, her gray head moving from side to side, her pale gray eyes uncertain. "But no matter what you do, here comes September," she said. "So tear August off the calendar!"

"Can I have August?" Tom stood holding the torn month in his hands.

"I don't know what you'll do with it," said Grandma.

"It isn't really over, it'll *never* be." Tom held the paper up. "I know what happened on every day of it."

"It was over before it began." Grandma's eyes grew remote. "I don't remember a thing that happened."

"On Monday I roller-skated at Chessman Park; on Tuesday I had chocolate cake at home; on Wednesday I fell in the crick." Tom put the calendar in his blouse. "That was this week. *Last* week I caught crayfish, swung on a vine, hurt my hand on a nail, and fell off a fence. That takes me up until last Friday."

"Well, it's good somebody's doing *some* thing," said Grandma.

"And, I'll remember today," said Tom, "because the oak leaves turned all red and yellow and fell down and I made a big fire out of them. And this afternoon I'm going to Colonel Quartermain's for a big birthday party."

"You just run and play," said Grandma. "I've got this job in the attic."

She was breathing hard when she climbed into the musty garret. "Meant to do this last spring," she murmured. "Here it is coming on winter and I don't want to go all through the snow, thinking about this stuff up here." She peered about in the attic gloom, saw the huge trunks, the spider webs, the stacked newspapers. There was a smell of ancient wooden beams.

She opened a dirty window that looked out on the apple trees far below. The smell of autumn came in, cool and sharp.

"Look out below!" cried Grandma, and began heaving old magazines and yellow trash down into the yard. "Better than *carrying* it downstairs."

Old wire frame dressmaker's dummies went careening down, followed by silent parrot cages and riffling encyclopaedias. A faint dust rose in the air and her heart was giddy in a few minutes. She had to pick her way over to sit down on a trunk, laughing breathlessly at her own inadequacy.

"More stuff, more junk!" she cried. "How it *does* pile up. What's *this* now?"

She picked up a box of clippings and cut-outs and buttons. She dumped them out on the trunk top beside her and pawed through them. There were three neat small bundles of old calendar pages clipped together.

"Some more of Tom's nonsense," she sniffed. "Honestly, that child! Calendars, calendars, saving calendars."

She picked up one of the calendars and it said OCTOBER, 1887. And on the front of it were exclamation marks and red lines under certain days, and childish scribbles: "This was a *special* day!" or "A *wonderful* day!"

She turned the calendar over with suddenly stiffening fingers.

In the dim light her head bent down and her quiet eyes squinted
to read what was written on the back:

"Elizabeth Simmons, aged 10, low fifth in school."

She held the faded calendars in her cold hands and looked
at them. She looked at the dates and the year and the exclamation marks and red circles around each special day. Slowly
her brows drew together. Then her eyes became quite blank.
Silently she lay back where she sat on the trunk, her eyes looking out at the autumn sky. Her hands dropped away, leaving
the calendars yellow and faded on her lap. July 8th, 1889
with a red circle scribbled round it! What had happened on
that day? August 28th, 1892; a blue exclamation point! Why?
Days and months and years of marks and red circles, and that
was all.

She closed her eyes and her breathing came swiftly in and out
of her mouth.

Below, on the brown lawn, Tom ran, yelling.

Miss Elizabeth Simmons aroused herself after a time, and got
herself over the window. For a long moment she looked down at
Tom tumbling in the red leaves. Then she cleared her throat and
called out, "Tom!"

"Grandma! You look so funny in the attic!"

"Tom, I want you to do me a favor!"

"What is it?"

"Tom, I want you to do me the favor of throwing away that
nasty old piece of calendar you're saving."

"Why?" Tom looked up at her.

"Well, because. I don't want you saving them any more," said
the old woman. "It'll only make you feel bad later."

"When, Grandma? How? I don't understand!" cried Tom back
up at her, hurt. "I've just got to keep every week, every month.
There's so much happening, I never want to forget!"

Grandma looked down and the small round face looked up
through the empty apple tree branches. Finally Grandma sighed,
"All right." She looked off. She threw the box away through the

autumn air to thump upon the ground. "I guess I can't make you stop collecting if you really want to."

"Thanks, Grandma!" Tom put his hand to his breast pocket where the month of August was tucked. "I'll never forget today, I'll *always* remember, I know!"

Grandma looked down through the empty autumn branches stirring in the cold wind. "Of course you will, child, of course you will," she said.

ARRIVAL AND
DEPARTURE

N O DAY IN all of time began with nobler heart or fresher spirit. No morn had ever chanced upon its greener self as did this morn discover spring in every aspect and every breath. Birds flew about, intoxicated, and moles and all things holed up in earth and stone, ventured forth, forgetting that life itself might be forfeit. The sky was a Pacific, a Caribbean, an Indian Sea, hung in a tidal outpouring over a town that now exhaled the dust of winter from a thousand windows. Doors slammed wide. Like a tide moving into a shore, wave after wave of laundered curtains broke over the piano-wire lines behind the houses.

And at last the wild sweetness of this particular day summoned forth two souls, like wintry figures from a Swiss clock, hypnotized, upon their porch. Mr. and Mrs. Alexander, twenty-four months locked deep in their rusty house, felt long-forgotten wings stir in their shoulder-blades as the sun rekindled their bones.

"Smell *that!*"

Mrs. Alexander took a drink of air and spun to accuse the house. "Two years! One hundred sixty-five bottles of throat molasses! Ten pounds of sulphur! Twelve boxes of sleeping pills! Five yards of flannel for our chests! How much mustard-grease? Get away!" She pushed at the house. She turned to the spring day, opened her arms. The sun made teardrops jump from her eyes.

They waited, not yet ready to descend away from two years of nursing one another, falling ill time and again, accepting but never quite enjoying the prospect of another evening together after six hundred of seeing no other human face.

"Why, we're strangers here." The husband nodded to the shady streets.

And they remembered how they had stopped answering the door and kept the shades down, afraid that some abrupt encounter, some flash of bright sun might shatter them to dusty ghosts.

But now, on this fountain-sparkling day, their health at last miraculously returned, old Mr. and Mrs. Alexander edged down the steps and into the town, like tourists from a land beneath the earth.

Reaching the main street, Mr. Alexander said, "We're not so old; we just *felt* old. Why, I'm seventy-two, you're only seventy. I'm out for some special shopping, Elma. Meet you here in two hours!"

They flew apart, rid of each other at last.

NOT HALF a block away, passing a dress shop, Mr. Alexander saw a mannequin in a window, and froze. There, ah, there! The sunlight warmed her pink cheeks, her berry-stained lips, her blue-lacquer eyes, her yellow-yarn hair. He stood at the window for an entire minute, until a live woman appeared suddenly, arranging the displays. When she glanced up, there was Mr. Alexander, smiling like a youthful idiot. She smiled back.

What a day! he thought. I could punch a hole in a plank door. I could throw a cat over the court house! Get out of the way, old man! Wait! Was that a *mirror*? Never mind. Good God! I'm really alive!

Mr. Alexander was inside the shop.

"I want to buy something!" he said.

"What?" asked the beautiful saleslady.

He glanced foolishly about. "Why, let me have a scarf. That's it, a scarf."

He blinked at the numerous scarves she brought, smiling at him so his heart roared and tilted like a gyroscope, throwing the world out of balance. "Pick the scarf you'd wear, yourself. That's the scarf for me."

She chose a scarf the color of her eyes.

"Is it for your wife?"

He handed her a five dollar bill. "Put the scarf on." She obeyed. He tried to imagine Elma's head sticking out above it; failed. "Keep it," he said, "it's yours." He drifted out the sunlit door, his veins singing.

"Sir," she called, but he was gone.

WHAT MRS. Alexander wanted most was shoes, and after leaving her husband she entered the very first shoe-shop. But not, however, before she dropped a penny in a perfume machine and pumped great vaporous founts of verbena upon her sparrow chest. Then, with the spray clinging round her like morning mist, she plunged into the shoe store, where a fine young man with doe-brown eyes and black-arched brows and hair the sheen of patent leather pinched her ankles, feathered her in-step, caressed her toes and so entertained her feet that they blushed a soft warm pink.

"Madame has the smallest foot I've fitted this year. Extraordinarily small."

Mrs. Alexander was a great heart seated there, beating so loudly that the salesman had to shout over the sound:

"If madam will push down!"

"Would the lady like another color?"

He shook her left hand as she departed with three pairs of shoes, giving her fingers what seemed to be a meaningful appraisal. She laughed a strange laugh, forgetting to say she had not worn her wedding band, her fingers had puffed with illness so many years that the ring now lay in dust. On the street, she confronted the verbena squirting machine, another copper penny in her hand.

M R. ALEXANDER strode with great bouncing strides up and down streets, doing a little jig of delight on meeting certain people, stopping at last, faintly tired, but not admitting it to anyone, before the United Cigar store. There, as if seven hundred odd noons had not vanished, stood Mr. Bleak, Mr. Grey, Samuel Spaulding and the Wooden Indian. They seized and punched Mr. Alexander in disbelief.

"Alex, you're back from the dead!"

"Coming to the Lodge tonight?"

"Sure!"

"Oddfellows meet tomorrow night?"

"I'll be there!" Invitations blew about him in a warm wind. "Old friends, I've *missed* you!" He wanted to grab everyone, even the Indian. They lit his free cigar and bought him foamy beers next door in the jungle color of green-felt pool tables.

"One week from tonight," cried Mr. Alexander, "open house. My wife and I invite you all, good friends. Barbeque! Drinks and fun!"

Spaulding crushed his hand. "Will your wife mind about tonight?"

"Not Elma."

"Fine!"

And Mr. Alexander was off like a ball of Spanish moss blown on the wind.

A FTER SHE left the store Mrs. Alexander was discovered in the streets of the town by a sea of women. She was the center of a bargain sale, ladies clustering in twos and threes, everyone talking, laughing, offering, accepting, at once.

"Tonight, Elma. The Thimble Club."

"Come pick me up!"

Breathless and flushed, she pushed through, made it to a far curb, looked back as one looks at the ocean for a last time before going inland, and hustled, laughing to herself, down the avenue, counting on her fingers the appointments she had in the next week at the Elm Street Society, the Women's Patriotic League, the Sewing Basket, and the Elite Theatre Club.

The hours blazed to their finish. The court house clock rang once.

Mr. Alexander stood on the street corner, glancing at his watch doubtfully and shaking it, muttering under his breath. A woman was standing on the opposite corner, and after ten minutes of waiting, Mr. Alexander crossed over. "I beg your pardon, but I think my watch is wrong," he called, approaching. "Could you give me the correct time?"

"John!" she cried.

"Elma!" he cried.

"I was standing here all the time," she said.

"And I was standing over there!"

"You've got a new suit!"

"That's a new dress!"

"New hat."

"So is yours."

"New shoes."

"How do *yours* fit?"

"Mine hurt."

"So do mine."

"I bought tickets for a play Saturday night for us, Elma! And reservations for the Green Town picnic next month! What's that perfume you're wearing?"

"What's that cologne *you've* got on?"

"No *wonder* we didn't recognize each other!"

They looked at one another for a long time.

"Well, let's get home. Isn't it a beautiful day?"

They squeaked along in their new shoes. "Yes, beautiful!" they both agreed, smiling. But then they glanced at each other out of the corners of their eyes and suddenly looked away, nervously.

Their house was blue-dark; it was like entering a cave after the fresh green spring afternoon.

"How about a little lunch?"

"Not hungry. You?"

"Me neither."

"I sure like my new shoes."

"Mine, too."

"Well, what'll we do the rest of the day?"

"Oh, go to a show maybe."

"After we rest awhile."

"You're not *tired*!"

"No, no, no," she cried, hastily. "You?"

"No, no!" he said, quickly.

They sat down and felt the comfortable darkness and coolness of the room after the bright, glaring warm day.

"I think I'll just loosen my shoelaces a bit," he said. "Just untie the knots a moment."

"I think I'll do the same."

They loosened the knots and the laces in their shoes.

"Might as well get our hats off!"

Sitting there, they removed their hats.

He looked over at her and thought: forty-five years. Married to her forty-five years. Why, I can remember…and that time in Mills Valley…and then there was that other day…forty years ago we drove to…yes…yes. His head shook. A long time.

"Why don't you take off your tie?" she suggested.

"Think I should, if we're going right out again?" he said.

"Just for a moment."

She watched him take off his tie and she thought: it's been a good marriage. We've helped each other; he's spoon-fed, washed and dressed me when I was sick, taken good care…Forty-five years now, and the honeymoon in Mills Valley—seems only the day before the day before yesterday.

"Why don't you get rid of your ear-rings?" he suggested. "New, aren't they? They look heavy."

"They *are* a bit." She laid them aside.

They sat in their comfortable soft chairs by the green baize tables where stood arnica bottles, pellet and tablet boxes, serums, cough remedies, pads, braces and foot-rubs, greases, salves, lotions, inhalants, aspirin, quinine, powders, decks of worn playing cards from a million slow games of blackjack, and books they had murmured to each other across the dark small room in the single faint bulb light, their voices like the motion of dim moths through the shadows.

"Perhaps I can slip my shoes *off*," he said. "For one hundred and twenty seconds, before we run out again."

"Isn't right to keep your feet boxed up all the time."

They slipped off their shoes.

"Elma?"

"Yes?" She looked up.

"Nothing," he said.

They heard the mantel clock ticking. They caught each other peering at the clock. Two in the afternoon. Only six hours until eight tonight.

"John?" she said.

"Yes?"

"Never mind," she said.

They sat.

"Why don't we put on our woolly slippers?" he wondered.

"I'll get them."

She fetched the slippers.

They put them on, exhaling at the cool feel of the material. "Ahhhhh!"

"Why are you still wearing your coat and vest?"

"You know, new clothes *are* like a suit of armor."

He worked out of the coat and, a minute later, the vest.

The chairs creaked.

"Why, it's four o'clock," she said, later.

"Time flies. Too late to go out now, isn't it?"

"Much too late. We'll just rest awhile. We can call a taxi to take us to supper."

"Elma." He licked his lips.

"Yes?"

"Oh, I forgot." He glanced away at the wall.

"Why don't I just get out of my clothes into my bathrobe?" he suggested, five minutes later. "I can dress in a rush when we stroll off for a big filet supper on the town."

"Now, you're being sensible," she agreed. "John?"

"Something you want to tell me?"

She gazed at the new shoes lying on the floor. She remembered the friendly tweak on her instep, the slow caress on her toes.

"No," she said.

They listened for each other's hearts beating in the room. Clothed in their bathrobes, they sat sighing.

"I'm just the *least bit* tired. Not too much, understand," she said, "just a *little bit.*"

"Naturally. It's been quite a day, quite a day."

"You can't just *rush* out, can you?"

"Got to take it easy. We're not young any more."

"That's right."

"I'm slightly exhausted, too," he admitted, casually.

"Maybe," she glanced at the clock, "maybe we should have a bite *here* tonight. We can always dine out tomorrow evening."

"A really smart suggestion," he said. "I'm not ravenous, anyway."

"Strange, neither am I."

"But, we'll go to a picture later tonight?"

"Of *course!*"

They sat munching cheese and some stale crackers like mice in the dark.

Seven o'clock.

"Do you know," he said, "I'm beginning to feel just a trifle queasy?"

"Oh?"

"Back aches."

"Why don't I just rub it for you?"

"Thanks. Elma, you've got fine hands. You understand how to massage; not hard, not soft—but just *right*."

"My feet are burning," she said. "I don't think I'll be able to make it to that film tonight."

"Some other night," he said.

"I wonder if something was wrong with that cheese? Heartburn."

"Did *you* notice, too?"

They looked at the bottles on the table.

Seven-thirty. Seven-forty-five o'clock.

"Almost eight o'clock."

"John!" "Elma!"

They had both spoken at once.

They laughed, startled.

"What is it?"

"You go ahead."

"No, you first!"

They fell silent, listening and watching the clock, their hearts beating fast and faster. Their faces were pale.

"I think I'll take a little peppermint oil for my stomach," said Mr. Alexander.

"Hand me the spoon when you're done," she said.

They sat smacking their lips in the dark, with only the one small moth-bulb lit.

Tickety-tickety-tick-tick-tick.

They heard footsteps on their sidewalk. Up the front porch stairs. The bell ringing.

They both stiffened.

The bell rang again.

They sat in the dark.

Six more times the bell rang.

"Let's not answer," they both said. Startled again, they looked at each other, gasping.

They stared across the room into each other's eyes.

"It can't be anyone important."

"No one important. They'd want to talk. And we're tired, aren't we?"

"Pretty," she said.

The bell rang.

There was a tinkle as Mr. Alexander took another spoonful of peppermint syrup. His wife drank some water and a white pill.

The bell rang a final, hard, time.

"I'll just peek," he said, "out of the front window."

He left his wife and went to look. And there, on the front porch, his back turned, going down the steps was Samuel Spaulding. Mr. Alexander couldn't remember his face.

Mrs. Alexander was in the other front room, looking out of a window, secretly. She saw a Thimble Club woman walking along the street now, turning in at the sidewalk, coming up just as the man who had rung the bell, was coming down. They met. Their voices murmured out there in the calm spring night.

The two strangers glanced up at the dark house together, discussing it.

Suddenly, the two strangers laughed.

They gazed at the dim house once more. Then the man and the woman walked down the sidewalk and away together, along the street, under the moonlit trees, laughing and shaking their heads and talking until they were out of sight.

Back in the living room Mr. Alexander found his wife had put out a small washtub of warm water in which, mutually, they might soak their feet. She had also brought in an extra bottle of arnica. He heard her washing her hands. When she returned from the bath, her hands and face smelled of soap instead of spring verbena.

They sat soaking their feet.

"I think we better turn in these tickets we bought for that play Saturday night," he said, "and the tickets for that benefit next week. You never can tell."

"All right," she said.

The spring afternoon seemed like a million years ago.

"I wonder who that was at the door," she asked.

"I don't know," he said, reaching for the peppermint oil. He swallowed some. "Game of blackjack, missus?"

She settled back in her chair with the faintest wriggle of her body.

"Don't mind if I do," she said.

THE BEAUTIFUL LADY

I T SEEMED THERE was never a time when someone did not say, "There was the Rose of Sharon, there was the lilies of the valley." "She walked like a princess. She could walk across the sands by the lake and the smallest breeze would blow the footprints away, she made so little mark in passing." The voices moved with the calendar through his life. "Have you ever put your head down in a bed of mint-leaves in May?" "In the middle of the hottest summer night you ever knew, have you felt the curtains blow out into your room, cool and white, suddenly. And the first rain falling on the hot night roof over your head?" They went all around and over and about the beautiful lady, trying to describe what it was about her. "It's like trying to tell you what red looks like, or blue, with your eyes shut." But they never gave up trying.

"She couldn't have been as beautiful as all that," cried George Gray. "Show us a picture of her!"

"That's fifty years ago," they said. "I suppose if you search around town you'll find one, but it's doubtful. She died young. It seems the whole town turned out for her, she was only nineteen and unmarried, when she died. I think everyone was in love with the girl, she was that special."

George Gray was alternately enchanted and in a rage with his elders. "Well, is she like Helen there, passing?" He pointed.

They only shook their heads with the faintest allowable degree of smugness. They had been to London, they had seen the queen. He had only been to Chicago, poor boy, and to Kankakee.

"Now there's a lovely girl, really lovely," said George, and he nodded to someone named Susanna passing in a car.

"That's a flower without scent," observed the old people. "So many girls today are flowers like that. When you touch them you find they're made of paper, to *last*. Alice wasn't made to last; she was like the first snow. You look out one December morning and it's falling but you never see it touch. It never covers the grass, it never has and never will."

"Oh, my God!" said George. "Shut up with this talk!"

He was only twenty, and hopelessly involved with every woman who sat rocking on a porch as he passed, or waved from a bus going by. He was always turning in circles and colliding with trees. He had fallen down several hypothetical elevator shafts and hit bottom a half dozen times, and still not found the woman he was looking for. There was a freckle on each, the nose was too long or the ear too large, or the mouth too open most of the time and making noise.

"All very well for you to talk," he said. "Memory plays tricks. It doubles and redoubles, it *squares* things for you. Why if Alice Langley strolled by on that sidewalk right now, you wouldn't know her."

"That's like saying," said old man Pearce, "I wouldn't know a certain species of transparent butterfly. Have you ever seen one, brought up from the Mexican rain-forests, the wings look like they were cut from blown glass, from crystal, you can see through them. When the butterfly sits on a flower it is a flower, when the butterfly sits on a peach it is a peach, there's nothing of the butterfly at all, except what you see through and beyond its wings. Don't tell me what I have or have not seen, young man, I have seen the butterfly with the crystal wings and you have not. Now, come on, let's have a game of chess."

G EORGE GRAY was alternately seized with paroxysms of despair and hatred. He wanted very much to see this rose, this butterfly, this first falling of the snows of winter, for he admired, above all else, beauty. If this woman was as they said she was, oh God to have a look at her! But this was patently impossible, the peach was harvested, the apple blossoms blown off in a wind that had failed fifty years before. You might just as well chase the rain with a sieve! And so his passion turned from despair to hatred and that variety of scorn best practised by a man only recently turned twenty. "A pack of lies!" he cried. "And fifty-two cards in the pack, all *marked*!"

"All except the Queen of Hearts," said old man Pearce. "Not a mark on her, not a spot, not a smirch," and lit his pipe.

"I'll prove she wasn't that beautiful!" cried George.

"How!"

"By her pictures, if I can find them! If you haven't burnt them, to cover up your story!"

"Lad," said Mr. Pearce. "Two thousand people don't show up at a maiden lady's funeral for no reason at all. People only show up in this world for things like the following: the golden spike being driven in the last tie of a railroad, the inauguration of a president, a man flies the Atlantic alone. They turn up for single events, lonely things, apart things, separate things, for things that are one of a kind and never another like it. She was one of a kind, lad, so why don't you let her be, eh?"

"I'll prove she wasn't as beautiful as you say, it's just you who were young and a fool, like myself," said George.

"Part of what you just said is wisdom," admitted the old man. "The last part."

"If I have to go out to where's she buried and dig her up and see for myself," said George.

The old man let his pipe die out. After a long while of sitting in the summer night he said, "George, George. You're cruel. They say youth is cruel. But this is the first time I've seen it this close.

Oh, but you are mean, aren't you? What's got you so mean this year? Is it breaking up with Susanna last month?"

"I'm not mean, I'm just practical," said George, lighting a cigarette.

"When a man talks as you just talked it's all the mean things ever was. Don't let me hear you speak again of bothering Miss Alice. Oh, that's a foul and awful thing to suggest, that's ghoul's talk, that's unhealthy. And besides—unfair. What can you find in a coffin anyway, but the seed of the plum, the skin left behind by a departed coral-snake, so much chaff and husk. There's a great difference between a wheat field in August with the sun and wind, and walking through the straw stubble in November. Is that how you'd judge a crop and a harvest, unfair like that?"

"I just want to prove you wrong," said George.

"You're a child," said Mr. Pearce, "in the body of a man. Why don't you fall down and kick on the floor?"

"I'll find a way," said George, smoking quietly and hastily. "I'll find a way, so help me."

"George," said the old man, sitting there by his chessboard. "I wish you'd go away now. I don't want to play another game tonight with someone like you. The heat's got hold of you for sure. Your talk's bad. Come back when you clean it up. A good walk in a hard rain would work wonders for you. Good night."

"You're afraid," and George smiled quietly. "You're afraid I'll take her away from you, aren't you. You're afraid of the facts, you're afraid I can find proof she was never what she seems to be now. I've got you running. I've got you scared."

"Good night, George," said the old man, in the shadows, and his voice was very tired and he did not move.

"Good night," said George, going down the porch steps.

He whistled away down the streets, his hands in his pockets, his head back, pausing only now and again from his song to smile.

"COME ON, Jack, why not?"

"George, it's crazy."

"We don't have to tell anybody. For my own satisfaction."

"George, let go of it. For cry-yi. Whinnikers, George."

"It'll be a clear night, cool and warm both."

"That's dirty and nasty, it's not clean."

"Where's your spunk?"

"It ain't in digging up nice people, darn it!"

"Old people always braggin', they should stop that."

"Sometimes it's all they got, give 'em that, George. Take it easy. Why you want to take things away from them? They already got so much taken away, why take the last bit, can you *tell* me?"

THERE WAS nothing inside the great box.

Or, at first, there seemed to be nothing. And then the wind blew just a little bit and stirred a few things there. And George Gray stood looking down upon these few things and counted them and named them over to himself and remembered them for many years after, and the meanness went out of himself, he felt the meanness go from his eyes and from around his mouth and from the muscles in his jaws and his lips, and the meanness drain from the hard muscles under his ribs and in the tendons of his back as he bent there. He let all the meanness melt away as if he were standing in the rain in a suit made of tissue papers and the first wash made him naked.

For inside of the box were the following things:

A single delicate green fern, as soft as breathing. A sprig of fresh summer mint. One new August peach, with the bloom still warm in it. One single violet, purple and alive. A red rose. And one blade of green summer grass.

That was all.

These things were placed, the green fern so, the peach this way, the red rose that, the summer grass another way, to suggest a form and a shape and a being. And standing there, George Gray found time to enact in his imagination the entire elaborate afternoon just over, Mr. Pearce, and a half dozen other old men, and the keeper of this vast and quiet land inside the fence and the iron gate, taking turns in the sun, digging, planning, arranging, and burying again, and going off in the sun, spades on shoulders, smiling. Why? To make a convert of a disbeliever, to bring him into their clan, the last one in the town, the skeptic, the cynic. To stop his mouth, to stop his doubt, to put an end forever to his threat. He glanced at the chimney of the oven-house on the far side of this marbled field; the faintest trace of smoke still went up to the sky.

He took one last look at the flowers and the delicate green fern and the blade of grass. Then he closed the lid gently and began filling the earth in over it, working steadily and quietly.

It was midnight when he reached his street, walking. It was five after midnight when, in passing the old man's place, he heard his own name called. He went up to the porch.

"Hello, George," said the old man.

"Hello," said George, uncertainly.

"George," said the old man, after a pause. "Are you still feeling mean and cantankerous?"

"I feel just fine," said George.

"You changed your mind any since last time I seen you?" asked the old man. "What do you think now?"

George said, "She's beautiful. She's the most beautiful lady I've ever seen, so help me."

"That's what I like to hear, George," said the old man. "That's what I like to hear. Tell you what; you just trot on over tomorrow night for a little game of chess, eh?"

"Yes, sir."

"I'll beat the pants off you, son."

"Yes, sir."

"Well, good night, George."

"Good night, sir."

George went down the steps and away from the house and left the old man sitting there in the dark. He did not look back, but waved his hand quietly when he heard the old man call good night again, and as George opened the screen door at this own house, a moth flew up suddenly, with a very soft touch indeed, and brushed his face, and was gone so quickly that is almost seemed it had never been there.

LOVE POTION

ALONE THEY LIVED in their house, the two old
sisters, as quiet as spiders, as large as sofas, both of them,
stuffed with time and dust and snow. Walking by their
house at night you saw their faces, like porcelain plates
in the unlit windows, or you saw their hands put up to draw the
green shade. And you heard no noise inside, save the dry crackling
of newspapers. Miss Nancy Jillet and her sister Julia took their
air at four in the morning when the town was undercover, and
the only one who ever saw them was the policeman walking by
swinging his nightstick threateningly at his shadow which ran
away ahead of him down the lanterned street as he marched away
from the raw lonely light.

So it was not impossible, then, that on an evening in summer, unable to sleep, with lines in her forehead and perspiration
in a dew upon her upper lip, Alice Ferguson, out for a walk
around the block, and not afraid for the moon was out and
the town serene and beautiful, and she was aged eighteen and
nothing could happen to her, happened upon the Jillets, the
two old ladies, sitting in the milky dark of 2 a.m., with needley,
silver stars for eyes and fat porcelain hands across their pin-
cushion breasts rocking slowly in their asthmatic rocking chairs,
alone, alone.

At first, Alice Ferguson was quite startled, and then, remembering the tales of their solitary confinement within life, lifted her hand and called, "Good evening," across the lawn to the silvered porch.

After a time, one of the chairs stopped rocking and one of the sisters said, "Good morning."

Alice Ferguson laughed. "Of course, it is morning. Good morning, then."

The sisters nodded silently.

"It's a lovely night," said Alice Ferguson.

"You're Alice Ferguson," said one of the old women.

"Yes, how did you know?"

"And you're 18 years old."

"Yes," she replied, uncertainly.

"Come here, child," said Nancy Jillet, the oldest and fattest of the two, in shadow.

She crossed the soft moon lawn to the edge of the railinged porch and peered in at the two half-seen faces.

"And you're in love," said Nancy Jillet, in an awful whisper.

"How did you know?"

The sisters rocked and looked at each other wisely.

"How did you know?" demanded Alice Ferguson.

"And he doesn't love you." said Nancy Jillet.

"Oh," said Alice.

"And you're unhappy and out walking late tonight," said the other sister in an old voice.

Alice stood before them, her head sinking, her eyelids flickering.

"Never you mind, child, never you mind," whispered Nancy Gillet, uncrossing her arms from her amazing breast. "You came to the right place."

"I didn't come…"

"Sh, we'll help you."

Alice found herself whispering, also, they were a trio of black velvet and white ermine conspirators, half moon, half shadow, there at the center of the night.

"How?" she whispered.

"We'll give you a love potion."

"Oh, but…"

"A love potion, child, to take with you."

"I can't afford…"

"No money, child."

"I don't believe…"

"You will, child, you'll believe, when it works."

"I don't want to…"

"Bother us? No bother. It's right inside, isn't it?"

"Yes. Yes."

"I must be going."

"Stay just a moment." The sisters had stopped rocking altogether and were putting their hands out, like hypnotists or tight rope walkers, at her.

"It's late."

"You want to win him, don't you?"

"Yes."

"All right then. Directions on the bottle. Get it, sister." And a moment later, in and out of the house like a huge dream, the sister had gone and fetched the green bottle and it rested, glittering, on the porch railing. Alice reached up her hand in the moonlight. "I don't know."

"Try it," whispered Nancy Jillet. "Try it once, is all we ask. It's the answer to everything when you're 18. Go on."

"But, what's in it…"

"Nothing, nothing at all. We'll show you." And from herself, as if she were bringing forth part of her bosom, Nancy Jillet drew forth a wrapped kerchief. Opening this she spread it on the rail in the moonlight, where a smell of fields and meadows arose instantly from the herbs contained therein.

"White flowers for the moon, summer-myrtle for the stars, lilacs for the rain, a red rose for the heart, a walnut for the mind, for a walnut is cased in itself like a brain, isn't it, do you see? Some clear water from the spring well to make all run well, and a sprig of pepper-leaf to warm his blood. Alum to make his fear grow small. And a drop of white cream so that he sees your skin like a moonstone. Here they all are, in this kerchief, and here is the potion in the bottle."

"Will it work?"

"Will it work!" cried Nancy Jillet. "What else could it do but make him follow you like a puppy all the years of your life? Who else would know better how to make a love potion than us? We've had since 1910, Alice Ferguson, to think back and mull over and figure out why we were never courted and never married. And it all boils down to this here, in this kerchief, a few bits and pieces, and if it's too late for us to help ourselves, why then we'll help you. There you are, take it."

"Has anyone ever tried it before?"

"Oh, no child. It's not just something you give to everyone or make and bottle all the time. We've done a lot of things in our life, the house is full of antimacassars we've knitted, framed mottos, bedspreads, stamp collections, coins, we've done everything, we've painted and sculpted and gardened by night so no one would bother us. You've seen our garden?"

"Yes, it's lovely."

"But it was only last week, one night, on my seventieth birthday, I was in the garden with Julia, and we saw you go by late, looking sad. And I turned to Julia and said, because of a man. And Julia said, if only we could help her in her love. And I was fingering a rose bush at the time and I picked a rose and said, Let's try. So we went all around the garden picking the freshest flowers and feeling young and happy again. So there it is, Alice, rose-water to whirl his senses and mint-leaves to freshen his interest and rain-water to soften his tongue and a dash of tarragon to melt his heart. One, two, three drops and he's yours, in soda pop, lemonade or iced-tea."

"I DO LOVE you," he said.

"Now I won't need this," she said, taking out the bottle.

"Pour a little out," he said, "before you take it back, so it won't hurt their feelings."

She poured a little out.

She returned the bottle.

"DID YOU give him some?"

"Yes."

"Good, good, just wait and see."

"And now we'll take some."

"Will you? I thought it was only for men?"

"It is, dear. But just this once, tonight, we'll take some, too. And we'll have beautiful dreams and dream we're young again."

They drank from it.

In the very early morning, she awakened to the sound of a siren in the streets of the green town. Running to the window, she looked out and saw what everyone had seen a few minutes before and would remember for years afterward. Miss Nancy and Miss Julia Jillet sitting on their front porch, not moving, in the broad daylight, a thing they had never done before, their eyes closed, their hands dangling at their sides, their mouths agape strangely.

There was something about them, something that suggested sheaths from which the iron blade is gone. This, Alice Ferguson saw, and the crowd moving in, and the police, and the coroner, putting his hand up for the green bottle that glittered brightly in the sunlight, sitting on the rail.

T MEETING

I T WAS AN evening unlike any he could remember in all of his life. Very early, after the sun went down, and the air was incredibly fresh, he began to tremble, an inner, hidden trembling, of excitement, almost of waiting. He arrived at the depot amid the dispersal of buses, the routine, the pattern, the gas, acceleration, the brakes, and then he was out, in his own bus, the tremor still in him. There were no accidents, it was a clear night, little traffic, few passengers. He drove through the ocean-quiet streets, smelling the salt air and feeling that certain thing in the wind that spelled spring no matter where you were, no matter what you were doing.

He was thirty-eight or thirty-nine, the first faint recession of hair beginning on his brow, the first quilled pricklings of silver touching his temples, the first criss-crossed leather creases starting to fold the back of his neck. He rotated the driver's wheel now this way, now that, automatically, and it was eleven at night, a sultry hour, warm, a spring night, and the trembling all through his body. He found himself looking and searching everything with his eyes, taking a special pleasure in the lemon ice neon signs and the green mint neon signs, glad to be out of his small apartment, glad of this night routine.

At the end of his first run he walked down to the edge of

the sea for a cigarette and a nervous moment of looking at the phosphorescence in the water.

Looking at the ocean, he remembered a night long ago when someone explained the phosphorescence to him; millions upon billions of tiny animal lives were boiling there, seething, reproducing, bringing others like themselves into myriad life, and dying. And the glow of this love in spring caused the shoreline to burn green, and in places like red coals, along the beach as far north as San Francisco, they said, as far south as Acapulco, or Peru, who could say, who could tell?

With his cigarette finished he stood a moment more by the sea wall feeling the wind blow the smell of the old apartment house off his clothes. His hands, though he had washed them, still felt greasy from the deck of solitaire cards he had used most of the afternoon in his room.

He went back to his bus, started the motor and let it idle, humming to himself. The bus was empty, this run was an empty run through sleeping avenues. He talked and sang to himself, to spin out the hours, alone, passing through shadowed moon streets toward the hour when he could go home, fall into a lonely bed, sleep late, and start all over again tomorrow afternoon at four.

At the fourth stop he paused long enough to open all the windows on the empty bus and turn out all but a few lights. Then he let the night wind run like a summer river, sluicing through every lifted pane, making the bus roar like a blown sea-shell. And there was only moonlight to ride on, silver asphalt to float over on boulevards of milk and black-velvet shadow.

He almost went past the young woman at the seventeenth stop.

She was standing in the open, but he was so preoccupied with breathing and smiling to himself, that he ran the bus a good twenty yards beyond her and she had to run quietly to get on when he opened the door. He apologized, she dropped her money in the silver-sounding box and sat in the seat across from him where he could see her from the corner of his eyes, and in the overhead mirror. She sat quietly, in the dim light, her hands folded upon her lap, her knees and feet together, her head up, her hair blowing.

And he was in love with her.

It was as immensely simple as that. He fell in love with this woman, very young, sitting in the seat across from him, her face pale as a milk-flower, everything about her folded and pressed and cleanly neat. Her hair was dark and blew like smoke in the wind and she sat so calmly and complacently there, not knowing she was beautiful or very young. She had used some light perfume early in the evening and the night had blown a good deal of it away, but some still remained faintly on the air. She looked very happy, as if some great news had come into her life tonight, her face shone, her eyes sparkled, and she rode, swaying gently, occasionally putting out her hand to hold when he slowed for a corner.

"I love her," he thought, and was surprised. "It's ridiculous, but I love her."

He knew how her voice must be, very gentle and kind, and how she would be and act, anywhere, at any time. It was in her dark eyes and in the way her hands touched everything, with a careful consideration. And then the pale light in her face glowed out upon things, it did not burn in upon herself and feed upon herself. It nourished others. It illumined the bus. It reflected the world and himself.

"Do you know?" he thought to her image in the mirror. "I love you? Do you suspect?"

They rode in the summer streets, toward midnight.

A ND THEN he knew. Inside each man, though he did not know it, nor ever considered it, was the image of the woman he someday must love. Whether she was composed of all the music he had ever heard or all the trees he had ever seen or all the friends of his childhood, certainly no one could tell. Whether the eyes were his mother's, and the chin that of a girl cousin swimming in a summer lake twenty-five years ago, this was unknowable also.

But most men carried this image, like a locket, like a pearl-cameo, in their head a lifetime, taking it out only rarely, taking it out never, after marriage, afraid then to compare it to the reality. And most men never saw the woman they would love anywhere, in the dark theatre, in a book, or passing on the street. They saw her only after midnight when the city was asleep and the pillow was cool under their heads. And she was a composite of all dreams and all women and every moonlit night since the calendar began.

"SHALL I tell you now?" he thought. "Do I dare?"

Now she had closed her eyes and leaned back to think of how this evening had been to her.

"If only you knew," he thought, and then the panic grew in him. There were only nine more stops. Somewhere along the way she would ring the buzzer and step out into the night and be gone. Somewhere ahead he would have to cry out suddenly, or be silent, "My name is William Becket, what's yours? Where do you live? Can I see you again?"

Eight stops. She was shifting in her seat and watching the streets.

"My name is William Becket, and I love you," he thought.

She raised her hand to the cord.

"No," he thought.

THE BUZZER rang. She arose as he slowed the bus toward its stop. He could come back in the morning, of course, to this stop. He could stand here and wait for her to come by, and say to her...and say to her...

His face was jerking now, a bit, up toward the mirror, down toward the avenue and the moon was very lovely in the trees. He knew he could not come here in the morning.

He stopped the bus and she was waiting at the door. Waiting for him to open it. He paused a moment and said, "I—"

She half-turned and looked at him with her beautiful face, the face that was everything he had ever thought about at night walking by the sea, in his free time.

He pressed the air-release, the door hissed open, she stepped out and was walking in the leafy moonlight.

I don't even know her name, he thought, I never even heard her voice. He kept the door open and watched her move off down the dark street. I didn't even see if she was married, he thought.

He closed the door and started the bus off and away, very cold now, his hands trembling on the wheel, not quite able to see where he was driving. After a moment he had to stop again and put down all the windows, there was too much draught. Half an hour later, coming back along this same street, he was rushing his bus too fast, for the avenues were empty and there was only the moon and the empty bus behind his back, and he was hurrying, hurrying, thinking to himself, if I hurry I'll reach the sea and if I'm lucky, it all depends, there may be some phosphorescence left, and there'll be time for a smoke and a walk before I turn the bus around and come back empty through the empty town.

THE DEATH OF
SO-AND-SO

I N THE ROOM, the deaths came and went. They were on all lips, and in every eye. Coffee cake went in and down to feed the stomach that kept the lungs busy with the talk of death. Coffee was creamed in cups and sugar sweetened the spell of old mortality in the parlor room. The four people faced each other, eager with stories of who and how and why, with names, dates and figures, with conditions and fortitudes, with descriptions of agonies and midnight sweats, of sutures and fractures, of comas and trachomas.

Mrs. Hette lifted her fat well-fed hand with the coffee cake in it like the contents of a steam-shovel. She paused in the death agony of Mr. Joseph Lantry, her best friend. She widened her mouth, showed the gray gums of her false teeth, faintly rimed with a froth, and bit into that cake. Chewing, swallowing, her eyes ugly bright, she continued with each detail of Mr. Lantry's death. He had spat blood upon the ground. He had coughed, making the noise of a chimney flue during a winter storm, vacuous and empty and horrible. He had had the red leaf of mortality across his cheeks. Her voice went up, up. Then, with his death, she fell back in her chair, shaking her head, closing her eyes, not understanding life with her usual I-don't-understand-life voice. Raising her food to her mouth she rained clods and crumbs of earth and coffee cake down upon Mr. Lantry's coffin.

"Poor Mr. Lantry," said Mrs. Spaulding, across the dim room.

"Yes," said Mr. Spaulding.

"That's how it goes," said Mr. Hette, stirring his black coffee.

They all waited the proper interval. A little watch ticked inside Mrs. Hette; somehow she always knew the right interval before going on with something else. You had to lay the dead out properly, with words and silences, before you went on to the next, alphabetical or not. With a shuttering of eyes and a resting of hands about your coffee plate you showed that it was a subject of much solemnity and worry to you.

Mrs. Spaulding took advantage of the pause to offer more cake to everyone.

Mr. Hette sucked his pipe. "Do you know how long since we last seen you people? Twenty years. Traveling and all. When we hit town today we didn't think we'd find you robbers *alive!*" Everybody laughed; it was nice to frost death up a bit. "What's happened in town since we left?"

"Remember Bill Samuelson? *He* died."

"What of?"

"Pneumonia," said Mr. Spaulding.

"Diphtheria," said Mrs. Spaulding.

Mr. Spaulding looked at Mr. Hette. "Helen Ferry, Tom Foley, Henry Masterson, all *them* died."

"What ever happened to—ah—Alaine Phillips?" Mr. Hette looked cautiously from the corners of his eyes, at his wife. His wife's eyes snapped.

"Alaine Phillips?" said Mr. Spaulding. "Why, didn't you *hear?* She was divorced the spring after you married Lita here, and went away to Ohio."

"Oh," said Mr. Hette.

Mr. Hette's wife glared at him.

"Alaine died the next year, however," added Mr. Spaulding.

"What!" cried Mr. Hette.

Mrs. Hette smiled over at the wall briefly, taking out her hankie to tap her nose. The hankie made it hard for Mr. Hette to see her mouth now. He sat looking at the carpet.

Now the two women took up the brisk routine of names.

Gussie Soderstrom? Alive. Well! Berenice Holdridd? Dead. *Well!* Talita Martin? Dead! *Really?* There were gasps where ever someone had fallen away; little laughs and wonders where ever a tree still stood, leafed and healthy. Mildred Partridge! Lily Johnson? Elna Sundquist? Dead, dead, dead.

Mrs. Hette, in the person of one Sylvia Gamwell, wandered into a chain drug store, lifted pieces of poison cream pie to her mouth, went out to wait for a bus and dropped dead, necessitating an autopsy attended by Mr. Hette, and Mr. and Mrs. Spaulding. All organs were minutely examined and found to be so heavily tainted with that kind of poison from cream pies left long in the sun, that the organs gave off a phosphorescent aura, like the breath of a dragon. Mrs. Hette's simulation of Miss Gamwell's death agony was something that brought everybody out to the edge of the sofa.

"It sure don't pay to eat in them chain drugs," snapped Mrs. Hette.

"I bake my own pies," said Mrs. Spaulding. "I'd rather die at home and take the blame!"

"Oh-ho." Mrs. Hette put coffee in on top of her laugh. "My friend Elma made up some pickle relish at home. One day she was happy about her Wedding on Saturday, ten days later her fiancé was courting a new girl and sending flowers out to Green Lawn Interment Park."

One of the men said, "How's business with you, Will?"

"Good even in bad years," said the other. "People got to smoke."

"Why, I got sick once just from drinking water," said Mrs. Hette. "Did you ever peek in a school microscope? In one water drop there's a million things. Every time you turn the kitchen faucet ten billion of them things drop out in your glass."

Now they were done with the actual deaths. The time of measurement was at hand. All of the *live* people in town would be weighed and found wanting. Estimates would be given as to how long before Mr. Talmadge died, Nancy Gillette died, or Eleanor Swift passed on? Those three were all so much bone dry kindling, their mouths askew with palsy, their hands cool if they touched you. They held Mr. Talmadge up, like the weight-guessing men at the carnival. "I'd say he'll live to be—ah—live to be—well… seventy, *no!* seventy-*five* years old!" Mrs. Hette closed her eyes disdainfully. "My dear, he'll fall downstairs one day and it'll be like when you fling a light bulb against a wall. That's him; brittle as *that!* He won't live another six months. Neither will Nancy Gillette, I saw *her* today, too!"

They rushed on to the anonymous dead. Finishing estimates as to the death time of their own living friends, they hurried on to people who were dying all across the land.

Planes crashed in the parlor. Trains toppled like timbers aflame. There were silent screams and tortures as the men sat idle-smoking their fresh-unwrapped cigars. Never ducking, the men sat flat-flanked in their chairs as cars splintered at their elbows and passengers were flung to hit the walls with soft, swift impact.

"Charred beyond recognition—"

"Crossing the tracks and she fell—Train ran over her—Picked her up in a basket—"

"Woman in Mellin Town—Husband came home—Found her in bed— Another man— Shot them and himself—"

While the women mingled their gasping breaths like perfumes, the men calmly carried out their direct, eye to eye, gray-frost talk of friends. "Remember Charlie Nesbitt who threw the burned mattress from the Clark Hotel at the Elk's Convention? He died last year." "Not old *Charlie!*" They stared at each other. "And here *we* are, still alive. Whatta you know?"

The women shuddered, clucked and laughed half-hysterically at what a world it was. They turned over several automobiles together, shook out the contents, examined them. They played detective, putting together a foully raped and dissected woman like a Chinese puzzle. After each subject they washed out their mouths with coffee and started fresh.

And finally, when the momentum died and the coffee pot was empty, they spiraled around and around to finally touch the subject to which they had been leading all through the autumn evening.

Themselves. How were *they* feeling?

Oh, Mrs. Hette *still* had her gallstones, but was bearing up.

Mrs. Spaulding was having *her* trouble too. She just *knew* she had stomach cancer. Was *Mister* Hette all right?

Mr. Hette's back *bothered* him.

Oh, Mr. Spaulding's back hurt *him* something awful, too. Some mornings he didn't rise until *nine*!

Well—Mrs. Hette smiled her triumph—Mr. Hette didn't get up until *NOON*!

"Of course," Mrs. Spaulding fixed her hair. "I imagine Leonard and I'll live to be old *old* people. We've a good family record for it."

"So have we," said Mrs. Hette instantly.

Mrs. Spaulding ticked her fingers. "My mother died at eighty-five, my father at ninety—"

"I thought you said he died at sixty-three?"

"Who?" Shrilly. "Father?" A laugh. "Ho, not *him*! Brisk as bacon at ninety!"

"Which one was it was an *invalid* from sixty on?"

"Invalid?" The blank surprise in Mrs. Spaulding's eyes. "Oh. You must mean cousin Wilma. *Third* cousin Wilma…"

"Now." Mrs. Hette moved her shoulders. "*All* my folks lived to be ninety. Same with Will's. We're liable to live a long, *long* time."

"I just hope we all have our *health*. It ain't no fun being old if you're sick. You'll be lucky if your gallstones don't kick up."

"I'm having them treated this month. And it's a matter of time before Will's back is cured. You ought to look into your *cancer*, also, Mrs."

"Heavens, it isn't cancer. Just gas, I know."

They sat regarding each other, one eye no brighter than another, hair about the same grayness, wrinkles in like profusion; all balanced, mentally, physically. Not liking it.

"Well, it's been nice." Mrs. Hette got up suddenly, not looking at her hostess. "Hope when we come back to town in five years you'll *still* be here." A stiff smile.

"You just be sure *you* come back." Drily.

The two men rose, smoking soft blue puffs of smoke, looking at each other with ancient soft warm eyes. They shook hands, slowly, tightly. "Well, Will?" "Well, Leo?" A hesitation. "Come back some time." They both looked at the floor. "If I don't see you again, well—be good." "Same to you."

"Lands, you'd think we were *old*, to hear you men talk!"

Everybody laughed. Coats were helped on, there was a hesitation and a number of farewells at the door, and some wavings when the Hette's car finally drove off down the dark midnight street.

The walls of the living room were yellow with the nicotine given off by the talk of death. The entire house was dim, cut off from the world, all the air sucked out under great pressure. Mr. and Mrs. Spaulding walked about the parlor in a little solemn merry-go-round of emptying ash trays, clearing dishes, and turning out the lights.

Mr. Spaulding went up the stairs without a sound save a kind of old engine coughing. He was already in bed when his wife arrived, exhilarated, and got in. She lay half smiling, glowing, in the dark.

Finally, she heard him sigh.

"I feel terrible," Leonard Spaulding said.

"Why?" she said.

"I don't know," he moaned. "I just don't feel good. Depressed."

"I'm sorry," she said.

"You and that damned Mrs. Hette. Christ, what an evening. Will, he's not so bad. But *her* and you. Christ, Christ, talk, talk!" He groaned in the dark room, all misery and ancient tiredness.

She tightened up. "We *never* have any one in any more."

"We're getting too old to have people in," he cried, faintly. "There's only one thing for old people to talk about, and you talked about it, by God, all evening!"

"Why, we didn't—"

"Shut up," he said, wearily, pleadingly, like a small withered child beside her. "I want to sleep."

They both lay for five minutes in the dark. She turned away from him, cold, stiff, her eyelids tight clenched. And just before her anger at him seeped away and sleep flooded down all through her like a drenching of warm rain, she heard two faint far women's voices talking one unto another, distantly, obscurely:

"My Will's funeral was the *finest* the town ever had. Flowers? Thousands! I *cried*. People? Everyone in *town*!"—"Well, you should have been at *Leonard's* funeral service. He looked so *fine* and natural, just like he was asleep. And *flowers*? Land! Banked around and banked around, and *people*!" — "Well, Will's service was" — "They sang 'Beautiful Isle of Somewhere.'" — "—people—" — "—flowers and—" — "—singing—"

The warm rain pattered over her. She slept.

I GOT SOMETHING YOU AIN'T GOT!

AGGIE LOU COULD hardly wait through the morning until Clarisse stopped in the house on the way home from school to lunch. Clarisse was the braided ten-year-old girl who lived next door and there was considerable rivalry between them.

Aggie Lou folded her body half out of the sunshiny window and called, "Clarisse, come up!"

"Why weren't you in school?" cried Clarisse, perturbed that her life opponent should be bedded down and taking it easy away from the grim school life.

"Come up and find out!" replied Aggie Lou, flopping back into bed.

Clarisse came upstairs quickly, a strap of books pendulumming in one grubby fist.

Aggie Lou lay back, eyes closed, pleased with herself. "I got something you ain't got," she revealed.

"What?" asked Clarisse suspiciously.

"Maybe I'll tell, maybe I won't," said Aggie Lou, lazily.

"I gotta go home and eat," said Clarisse, not taken in by this strategy.

"Then you'll never know what I got," said Aggie Lou.

"Well, what is it?" shouted Clarisse, scowling.

"Bacteria," announced Aggie Lou proudly.

Clarisse's eyebrows went down. "What?"

"Bacteria. Microbes. Germs!"

"Oh, poo!" Clarisse swung her books carelessly. "Everybody's got germs. I got germs, too. Looky." She displayed ten fingers, equally begrubbed and the furthest state from antiseptic.

"That's on the outside," criticized Aggie Lou. "I got my germs on the inside, where it counts!"

Clarisse was finally impressed. "Inside?"

"They're running around all over my machine, Dad says. Dad smiles funny when he says it. So does the doctor. They say I got them all over my lungs, having a regular picnic."

Clarisse looked at her as if she were some black-braided saint glowing in holy repose upon crisp linen. "Lordy."

"The doctor took some of my germs and put them under one of them seeing things and they ran around playing cops and robbers under his eyes. So there!"

Clarisse had to sit down. Her face was a little pale and flushed at the same time. It was easy to see that Aggie Lou's triumph had made inroads upon her peace of mind. This particular triumph was much bigger than Clarisse's Monarch butterfly which she had captured with a piggy squeal in her back yard last week and taunted Aggie Lou with. It was even the next size triumph over Clarisse's party dress, which was all ruffles and pink roses and ribbons. It was a factor over and above Clarisse's Uncle Peter who spat brown spit from a toothless mouth and had one wooden leg. Germs. Real germs, inside!

"So," finished Aggie Lou, controlling her triumph with admirable calm, "I won't go to school ever again. I won't have to learn arithmetic or anything!"

Clarisse sat there, defeated.

"And that ain't all," said Aggie Lou, holding back the best thing for the last.

"What else?" demanded Clarisse harshly.

Aggie Lou looked about her bedroom quietly, settling back

and worming into the blankets warm and nice. Then she said, "I'm going to die."

Clarisse leaped from her chair, hair bouncing in blonde startlement. "What?"

"Yes. I'm going to die." Aggie Lou smiled gravely. "So there, Smarty!"

"Oh, Aggie Lou, you're lying! You're a dirty fibber!"

"I'm not either! You just ask Mama or Papa or Doctor Nielson! They'll tell you! I'm going to die. And I'm going to have the nicest coffin ever. Dad said so. You should see Dad when he talks to me. Sometimes he comes in late at night and sits here, where you're sitting, and holds my hand. I can't see him very well, except his eyes. They're funny. He says lots of things. He says I'll have a coffin plated with gold, and satin inside, a regular doll house. He says I'll have dolls to play with. He says he's buying me some land of my own for my doll house where I can play all by myself, Smarty. It'll be on a hill where I can own the whole world just by looking at it, Dad said it, too. And, and, and I'll just play with my dolls and look pretty. I'm going to have a green party dress like yours, and a Monarch butterfly, and better than your Uncle Peter I'll have SAINT Peter for myself!"

Clarisse's face was tense with keeping back the jealous rage in her. Tears stood bold on her cheeks, and she rose undecided from her perch to stare at Aggie Lou.

Then, screaming fitfully, she plunged from the room, ran down the stairs, and out into the spring day, and across the green lawn to her house, sobbing all the way.

Clarisse slammed the door in upon herself and the kitchen cooking odors. Clarisse's mother was dissecting apples into a crust-lined tin and she declaimed against the door slamming.

"Oh, I don't care!" snuffled the little girl, sliding her pink bloomered bottom upon the built-in table bench. "That old Aggie Lou next door!"

Clarisse's mother looked up. "Have you two been at it again? How many times have I told you?—"

"Well, she's going to die, and she sits there in bed smiling at me, smiling at me. Gee!"

The mother dropped her knife. "Will you say that again, young lady?"

"She's going to die, and she sits there laughing at me! Oh, mother, what'll I do?"

"What'll you do? About it? Or what?" Bewilderment. The mother had to sit down, her fingers were jumping up and down on her apron.

"I've got to stop her, Mother! She can't get away with it!"

"That's awfully nice of you, Clarisse, being so thoughtful."

"I'm not being nice, Mama. I hate her, I hate her, I hate her."

"But I don't understand. If you hate her, why are you trying to help her?"

"I don't want to help her!"

"But you just said—"

"Oh, Mama, you don't help!" She cried bitterly and bit her lips.

"Honestly, you children. It's so hard to figure you out. Do you or don't you want to do something about Aggie Lou?"

"I do! I've got to stop her! She can't do it. She's so stuck up about her—germs! Clarisse pounded the table top. "She keeps singing 'I got something you ain't got!'"

Her mother exhaled. "Oh, I think I'm beginning to see."

"Mother, can I die? Let me die first. Let me get even with her, don't let her do this!"

"Clarisse!" A heart whirled like the egg-beater beneath the calico apron. "Don't you ever talk like that again! You don't know what you're saying! My land, oh, my land!"

"Why can't I talk like this? I guess I can talk if Aggie Lou can."

"Well, you don't know anything about death, in the first place. It's not like what you think it is."

"What is it like?"

"Well, it's—it's—well. Goodness, Clarisse, what a silly question. There's—nothing wrong with it. It's quite natural really. Yes, it's quite natural."

Her mother felt herself caught between two philosophies. The philosophy of children, so unknowing, so one-dimensional, and her own full-blown beliefs which were too raw, dark and all-consuming to descend upon the sweet little ginghamed things who skirted through their ten year era with soprano laughter. It was a delicate subject. And, as with many mothers, she did not take the realist's way out, she simply built upon the fantasy. Heaven knows it was easier to look on the bright side, and what little girls don't know can't hurt them. So she simply told Clarisse what Clarisse didn't *want* to hear. She told her, "Death is a long sweet sleep, with maybe different kinds of nice dreams. That's all it is."

Therefore she was dismayed when Clarisse broke into a new storm of rebellion. "That's the trouble! I'll never be able to talk to kids at school, after this. Aggie Lou'll laugh at me!"

The mother suddenly got up. "Go up to your room, Clarisse, and don't bother me. You can ask questions later, but for heavens sake leave me alone to think now! If Aggie Lou's going to die, I have to see her mother right away!"

"Will you do something to stop Aggie Lou from dying?"

The mother looked down into the child's face. There was no compassion or understanding there, just the bright ignorance and primitive jealousy and emotion of a child wanting something and not understanding what degree of something it wants.

"Yes," said the mother strangely. "We'll try to stop Aggie Lou from dying."

"Oh, thank you, Mother!" cried Clarisse in triumph. "I guess we'll show her!"

The mother smiled weakly, vaguely, closing her eyes. "Yes, I guess we will!"

MRS. SHEPHERD knocked at the back of the Partridge house. Mrs. Partridge answered. "Oh, hello, Helen."

Mrs. Shepherd murmured something and stepped into the kitchen, thinking to herself. Then when she was seated in the kitchen eating nook she looked up at Mrs. Partridge and said, "I didn't know about Aggie Lou."

The carefully assembled smile on Mrs. Partridge's face fell apart. She sat down, too, slowly. "I don't like to talk about it."

"No, of course you don't, but I've been wondering…"

"About what?"

"It seems silly. But somehow I think we've raised our children wrong. I think we've told them the wrong things, or else we haven't told them enough."

"I don't see what you mean," said Mrs. Partridge.

"It's just that Clarisse is jealous of Aggie Lou."

"But that seems so strange. Why should she be jealous?"

"You know how children are. Sometimes one of them gets something, something neither good nor bad nor worth wanting, and they build it into something shining and wonderful so all other children are jealous. Children have the most inexplicable methods of obtaining their ends. They promote jealousy with the most peculiar weapons, even Death. Clarisse doesn't really want—want to be sick. She just—well—she just thinks she does. She doesn't really know what Death is. She hasn't been touched by it. Our family has been lucky. Her grandparents and cousins and uncles and aunts are all alive. There hasn't been a death among us in twenty years at least."

Mrs. Partridge drew into herself, and turned over Aggie Lou's life as if it were a doll to be examined. "We've fed Aggie Lou on pretty dreams, too. She's so young, and now with the illness, well, we thought we would make it easier for her if anything should happen…"

"Yes, but don't you see that it's causing complications."

"It's making my daughter's life bearable. I don't know how she'd go on otherwise," said Mrs. Partridge.

Mrs. Shepherd said, "Well, I'm going to tell my daughter tonight that it's all nonsense, that she's not to believe one more word of it."

"But how thoughtless," came back Mrs. Partridge. "She would only rush over and tell Aggie Lou, and Aggie Lou would—well—it just wouldn't be right. You see?"

"But Clarisse is unhappy."

"She has her health, at least. She can bear being unhappy awhile. Poor Aggie Lou, she deserves what little joy she can find."

Mrs. Partridge had a good point and stuck to it. Mrs. Shepherd had to agree that it might be wise to let it go a while longer, "Except that Clarisse is so disturbed."

IN THE next few days from her window Aggie Lou saw Clarisse all dressed up and going down the street and when she called to ask over the distance where Clarisse was going, Clarisse pivoted and with a shining white look, which was alien to her face, replied that she was going to church to pray for Aggie Lou to get well.

"Clarisse, you come back here, come back!" shouted Aggie Lou.

"Why, Aggie Lou," said her parents to her, "how can you be so cross towards Clarisse, she's so considerate, bothering to go all the way to church that way."

Aggie Lou thumped over in bed, muttering into the pillow.

And when the new doctor appeared, Aggie Lou stared at him and his silver hypodermic and said, "Where'd he come from?"

The doctor, it turned out, was a cousin of Mr. Partridge's who had experimented with some new injections which he promptly gave to Aggie Lou with a smile and only a little prickling pain to her arm.

"I suppose Clarisse had something to do with this?" asked Aggie Lou.

"Yes, she kept talking to her father and her father finally telegraphed the doctor."

Aggie Lou rubbed her injection mark fiercely and said, "I knew it, I *knew* it!"

At night, in the cool darkness, Aggie knelt upon her bed and looked at the ceiling. "God, if you're listening to Clarisse, don't any more. She spoils everything. After all, it's up to me, isn't it, to ask for what happens to me? Yes. Then, don't pay no attention to Clarisse, she's mean. Thank you, God."

Late that night she tried her very hardest to die. She gritted her teeth and sweat rolled down and tasted of salt in her mouth. She clenched her fists and held them taut at her sides and stretched her body like a steel spring. Inside, she tried to catch the beat of her heart, using her ribs and lungs as hands to clutch it with and stop it, as you stop a clock in the night when its ticking keeps you awake.

Finally, too warm, she threw back the covers and lay moist and panting. Much later she went and stood by the window and looked over at the other house where the lights burned until dawn. She practiced lying on the floor and dying. And she practiced sitting in a chair and dying. She tried it in many postures, but nothing happened, her heart ticked merrily on.

At other times Clarisse would come stand under her window. "I'm going to jump in the river," she said, tauntingly. Or, "I'm going to eat until I bust."

"Shut up!" Aggie Lou would reply.

Clarisse would bounce her red ball and pass her little curve of leg over over over it, one two three four, over over. And while doing it she would sing, "Gonna jump in the river, gonna leap off a hotel, gonna eat till I bah-ust, gonna jump in the rih-ver." Bounce, bounce, bounce rubber.

Slam, would go Aggie Lou's windows!

Aggie Lou scowled in bed. Supposing Clarisse did what she said? It would be spoiled. There would be no use dying then. Aggie Lou hated to be second comer for anything. She always wanted something her very own. Clarisse had just better not try anything!

Then, the insidious thing began to take place. Aggie Lou started feeling better. The yellow sun looked bright, hot. The birds sang sweetly. She smelled the air like spring wine. But she was afraid to tell mother because mother would tell Clarisse and Clarisse would go ha ha oh ha ha, haha oh haha and yahhh for you! Aggie Lou realized, like a flash bulb going off, that she was getting well! Did the doctor know? Did mother guess? They mustn't. Not yet. No, not yet.

And she began to feel like running in the sun, over the lawns, she felt like hop scotching and climbing leafy trees, and lots of things. But she didn't dare say this. No, she pretended she was still sick and going to die. A weird thought came to her suddenly that she didn't really care about that silver house on the hill, or the dolls, or the dress, it was just so good not to feel tired.

But there was Clarisse to be faced, and what if she got well now and Clarisse teased her? My, she couldn't bear to think of it!

So next time Clarisse ran by like a pink robot on the grass, Aggie Lou yoohooed. "I'm going to die Thursday at three-fifteen. The doctor said so. He showed me a picture of my nice casket!"

And a few minutes later Clarisse rushed out of her house, her coat and bonnet on, heading down toward church to see what she could do to circumvent this!

And as she returned at twilight, Aggie Lou leaned out and said in a faint and poignant whisper: "I'm feeling worse!"

Clarisse stamped her foot.

THE NEXT morning a fly landed on the quilt. The fly walked around until Aggie Lou hit it. Then it lay quivering and then was silent. It didn't make a noise. It didn't buzz or twitch.

When father came up bearing breakfast on a tray she pointed at the fly and asked a question.

Her father nodded. "Yes, it's dead." He gave it no importance, he seemed preoccupied with something else. It was, after all, just a fly.

After breakfast, alone, she touched the fly and it did not protest.

"You're dead," she said. "You're dead."

An hour of watching and waiting revealed something to her. "Why, he doesn't do anything. Just sits there."

"How silly," she said, forty minutes later. "That's no fun."

And she looked over at Clarisse's house and then lay back, closing her eyes, and, presently, she began to smile, contentedly.

HOW IT came about three days later that Clarisse had her accident, no one knew. It happened for sure. After three days of Aggie Lou poking out the window, advising Clarisse as to her coming death, Clarisse ran to play softball in the street Wednesday afternoon with some other girls who played way out in the distances behind the boy fielders.

They were chasing long flies when the accident happened.

Homer Philipps smacked out a walloping three bagger and Clarisse ran to catch it and a car turned a sharp corner, and Clarisse was running along silently, when the car made her stop by hitting her.

Now, whether the car or Clarisse was to blame is one of those things you can talk about forever but never settle. Some say Clarisse didn't look around—others say she did, but something compelled her to keep running.

The car lifted her like a leaf and tossed her. She tumbled and broke.

AGGIE LOU'S mother came into her room that night.

"Aggie Lou, I want to talk to you about Clarisse."

"What about Clarisse?" asked Aggie Lou, breathlessly.

Two months later, Aggie Lou walked up to the cemetery hill and listened to Clarisse's silence and not moving, and dropped some worms on the grave to help things along.

THE WADERS

THE FEET WAITED inside the door, burning in their leather boxes. The feet waited inside a thousand doors and the day burned green and yellow and blue, the day was a great circus banner. The trees stamped their images fiercely upon clouds like summer snow. The sidewalks fried the ants and the grass quivered like a green ocean. And the feet waited, white with a winter of waiting, large and small feet, tender with six months of imprisonment, delicate and blunt feet, apprehensive and wiggling in warm darkness. And far and away and above came the muted and then the whining arguments about the season of the year, the temperature, colds, winter hardly over, or spring hardly over, rather. But this, said the whining voices, the insistent voices, was green summer, this was the day of the sun. And the feet worked their toes together and clenched the material of the socks in darkness, waiting.

There, just beyond the squeaking porch, the ferns were a green water sprinkled softly on the air. There waited the great pool of grass with its tender heads of clover and its devil weed, with its old acorns hidden, with its ant civilizations. It was toward this grass country that the feet were slowly inching. As the body of a boy on a sweltering July day yearns toward swimming holes, so the feet are drawn to oceans of oak-cooled grass and seas of minted clover and dew.

As the naked bodies of boys plunge like white stones and bobble like brown corks in the far country rivers, so the feet wish to plunge and swim in the summer lawns, refreshed.

Well, said a woman's voice, well. A screen door opened. All right, said the voice, all right, but if you catch your death of cold, don't come to me, sniffling.

Bang! Out the door! Over the rail! Watch the ferns! And into the lake of grass! Under the shady oaks! Off with the shoes, and now, running wet in the dew, running dry and cool under apple shade and oak shade and elm shade, a hot race over desert sidewalks, and the coolness of limes again on the far side, the touch of green ice and menthol, the feet burrowing like animals, feeling for old autumn's leaves buried deep, feeling for a year ago's burnt rose-petals, for anthills. The pompous, nuzzling big white toe, jamming into cool dark earth, the little toes picking at milky-purple clover buds, and now, just standing, the hot feet drowning in cool tides of grass. Time enough later, to venture tenderly out on cinder drives and rocky paths where the enemy, the shattered bottles, brown and glittering white, lie waiting to test one's softened calluses. Time enough later for these marshmallow, winter-soft feet to slim themselves like Indian braves, paint themselves with colored dirts, bruise themselves with rocks and thorns.

Now, now, just the cool grass. The cool grass and a thousand other bare feet, running and running there.

THE DOG

H E *WAS* THE town. He was the town compounded and reduced, refined to its essences, its odors and its strewing.

He walked through the town or ran through the town any hour of the day or night, whenever the whim took him, when the moon drew him with its nocturnal tides or the sun brought him like a carved animal from a Swiss clock. He was small; with a handle you could have carried him like a black valise. And he was hairy as copper-wool, steel-wool, shavings and brushes. And he was never silent when he could be loud.

He came home from the cold night lake with a smell of water in his pelt. He came from the sands and shook a fine dust of it under the bed. He smelled of June rain and October maple leaves and Christmas snows and April rains. He was the weather, hot or cold. He fetched it back from wherever he was, wherever he had been. The smell of brass; he had lounged against fire station poles amid intervals of tobacco spitting and come home feverish from political conversation. The smell of marble; he had trotted through the cool tombs of the court house. The smell of oil; he had lain in the cool lubrication pit at the gas station, away from summer. Frosted like a birthday cake he entered from January.

Baked like a rabbit he came in from July with world-shaking messages buried in his clock-spring hair.

But mostly he followed the Revolution; he moved in the sounds and shadowing of boys, and more often than not, his tongue slickly protruding in a smile, he wore a hand, like a white hat, moving, on his head....

THE RIVER THAT WENT TO THE SEA

EVERY NIGHT AFTER kissing mother, mashing her warm sweet hugeness into his small arms, and rubbing the abrasive cheek of father, so full of the odor of tobacco and machinery, he would run to the bathroom and stand enchanted with the secret note in his hand, poised, ready to send it on its way. And the note would read, "Dear Mermaid, I am Tom Spaulding and I live at 11 South Saint James in Green Town, Illinois and—"

Then he would press the toilet handle. The clear cool waters would gush with a throttling roar down the tile throat. At the very last moment, he would drop his secret note into the vanishing river. The waters would cease flowing. All would be quiet. The note was gone. He would stand for a moment thinking, It's going on down to the sea, now, way on down to the sea. And then he would go to bed. I wonder if she's reading it now, he thought, lying there. I wonder if she is.

OVER, OVER, OVER, OVER, OVER, OVER, OVER, OVER!

I N CHILDHOOD HE saw the yellow rubber ball flung over the topmost slats of the house, pause against the Illinois summer sky and come dribbling down the opposite side, while the children sang.

"Over, over, over! Over, Annie, over!"

Sometimes it sounded like a person calling a dog.

"Rover, rover, rover!" they cried. "Rover, any Rover?"

On the moist green lawn at seven in the evening when the distant clatter of dishes told of mother cleansing them in the house, as shadows were spread like carpets for them to sit on, they began to play the game.

"Pick a word?" asked Hilda, flopping her buttery coils of hair. "Umm." She squinched her nose until the freckles were lost. "How about 'storm'?"

The seven other children digested the word. They looked at each other with questions in their shadowsy eyes. "Yes," someone said. "Yes," everyone agreed. "Let's try *storm*."

"Storm, storm, storm, storm, storm, storm!" they cried. "Storm, storm, storm, storm, storm, storm, storm, storm, storm!"

Then they stopped abruptly, withheld their mirth a moment and one of them said, "What does that mean? Storm? Is it a word? It sounds so queer. That isn't a word at all!"

THE PROJECTOR

H E HAD THIS small motion picture projector hidden in his head and when he went to bed at night he ran films from the time the lights went out until his eyes closed and he could no longer see the oblong on the wall full of witches and castles and monsters and misty seas. He ran the films every night for years and nobody knew how talented he was. He never told a soul about his magnificent ability. It was better that way.

THE PEOPLE WITH
SEVEN ARMS

"IT CAME LATE," said Grandfather. "For Tom. It started early for you and it's still going on. Discovering things, looking at things, smelling, sniffing, tasting things. Hearing things. It should never stop. It stops for most people, but they shouldn't let it. Don't let it. Keep it up all your life. I do. I do keep it up every day. Like with the lawn, and the dandelion wine. See, hear, feel, touch, smell, know, and you love. Put out your hands. God gave you seven. Your two regular ones, plus nose, mouth, eyes, ears, skin.

"When you stop knowing you stop loving and when you stop loving you're not living, and when you're not living, Douglas boy, you might as well be dead."

A SERIOUS DISCUSSION
(or EVIL IN THE WORLD)

"**D**OUGLAS," SAID GRANDFATHER, "You must learn as soon as possible the difference between the real world and the world the way you would like it. The difference between the way some people teach us the world is, and the way it happens to be. For only then will you know what to expect, boy. You will see the world clear. And you won't be a cynic, a man with a bunch of dreams still lying around in the back of the mind, that turns him sour on everything. And you won't be a skeptic, either, really. I don't even know if there's a name for it, boy. You'll just be someone that looks at the world straight off and sees it. You can even enjoy the duplicity of man, somehow. By recognizing that evil is natural to man, you should be able to cope with it better."

THE FIREFLIES

"FIREFLIES NEVER QUITE make it back," said Grandfather, on the bottom front porch stair.

"Make it back where?"

"My father used to say they were stars got shaken loose. On summer nights, he said, God cleaned his furnace, shook it down. Coals dropping everywhere. Run out and pick up a few, he'd say. I'd run. Come back, a light in each hand."

"I'll catch some," said Douglas.

"Thanks."

Douglas moved like a breath. There was darkness and stars in the heavens and stars on the lawn.

"They don't even burn!"

"No. Gentle now."

"They've gone out!"

"Startled."

The fireflies were transferred to Grandfather's cupped hands. Later, they lit up again.

"I wish I could glow like that."

"Why, boy, you *do*. We all do, at times. Poets say love burns with a pure light. Here's proof. Anything as beautiful as this must be important."

"I don't light up like *that*."

"Saw you looking at your mother yesterday. In a dark room, bet I could read a book by your face."

"Aw."

"Yes, *sir!*" Grandfather held up the fireflies. "Better let them get back to brightening the corner where they are." He opened his hand. They lit the air softly, flying away. "Yes, sir, love is a wonderful thing."

"We go out in the lobby and eat popcorn or go to the toilet until its over, matinees."

"You've got yourself an argument."

"It's pretty silly, some Saturdays."

"You ever see Grandma and me on the movie screen down there?"

"Heck, no."

"Ever seen your mother, father, yourself, your brother on that screen?"

"Not yet."

"I'm afraid you never will. Or any of your friends or aunts or uncles, or the boarders here. On the day when the Elite theatre starts showing Grandma and me and your mother and father and all the other relatives and boarders, tell me, I'll come down with you. We'll stay until midnight and they sweep us out with the popcorn. In the meantime, Douglas, you keep right on marching to the restroom when things get silly on the screen. You've got good common sense in that head. Everybody knows love isn't like that."

"Charlie Henwood says he sure hopes not."

"Maybe you're wondering what it is, then? It's what I said; its you and me and Grandma and all our children and the children of uncles and cousins, and all the boarders here. It's how we all feel about each other most of the time, subtract the fights and meanness. Simple as that. It's trying to live peaceably in an un-peaceable world. It's Grandma baking a pumpkin pie and me whittling you a hickory whistle. It's you sitting here right now listening very politely. And you and your brother going to sleep winter nights and warming your feet, one on the other. It's your mother worrying when your father works late, and there may have been an accident. It's all of us laughing at the dinner table. It's Neva playing for us to sing in the parlor. It's sitting here on the porch nights, or a game of checkers in the fall, inside. It's so darned many things I can't tell them all. But it's a miracle if you find them on that silver screen downtown Saturday matinees. Almost as hard to find in the evening shows. Once a year maybe I see Grandma on the screen, or myself, or someone I know. The rest of the time it might as well be a bunch of rabbits hitting each other on the head with clubs, for all I understand the shows. Do you know why they put those kissing scenes in films? They can't think of anything to say that means anything. It's the trademark of an empty man. When they show you that sort of thing, Douglas, you just stroll right out of the theatre and stand on the nearest street-corner. You'll see more real love in the popcorn man's cat and her kittens than you'll ever buy for a dime at the show. Don't let it fool you. The kiss is just the first note of the first bar, played by a piccolo. What follows is either a symphony or a riot, everyone trying to get out the door."

"What good is love?"

"Good. Well, I guess you'd call it a kind of lubricant. It stops friction. There are so many elbows to knock and feet to step on in this world. And so many people swatting each other in the face with pan-cake flippers, accidentally, of course, you need to be baptized in this first-grade oil, love, or you wouldn't get anywhere. Your brakes would burn out on the first mile."

THE CIRCUS

THE EMPTY MEADOW lay beyond the town.

At eight o'clock, Tom Spaulding came walking through the dusk to the edge of the meadow and stood breathing in the scents that blew from the summer grass in whispers.

"This is where it was," he thought. "If only I could have come. If only I hadn't had a cold and stayed in bed."

He walked slowly to the center of the meadow. He stood sniffing, under the great chandelier of stars as all the blazing constellations caught fire and burned above him.

"Here's where the lions were…"

The yellow smell, the smell of carpeting in sunlight, the smell of African dust, the smell of violent acid. A few quartz pebbles glittered in the dry grass like yellow animal eyes, and turned to stone once more as he bent down.

"Here's where the elephants stood."

The wind was large, towering above him, touching him with a cold, wrapping-around touch. The wind swayed back and forth, invisible. And the smell of the elephant was like a huge barn.

"Here's where I'd have fed them."

He picked up a few scattered peanut-shells, shoved them in his pocket after looking them over and over.

"And here's where the monkeys were and the zebras and camels."
The dry bushes chattered in the wind. Summer lightning painted
great luminous stripes upon the hills, soft, pale, and gone.

There hadn't even been a circus parade. The lions had been
silenced outside of town by the Lions inside of town. The elephants
had been vanquished by the Elks. The calliope had been throttled
and choked with red-tape and the entire circus assemblage, band,
wagons, and clowns had fled before an Ark of Moose, Eagles and
Oddfellows. The Kiwanis, reaching out its arm for its proverbial
handshake, had had its knuckles slapped by Colonel Quartermain.
Quartermain, Quartermain, the name was an unending repetition
in the crowd of days, his face appeared in every window, on every
street, he spoke from every monument on Memorial morning,
he stood silent on Armistice Day facing East, he cried out from
between the tar-black Civil War cannons on the Fourth of July.
His eye was glittered at you from the clawing eagle's head on
the back of every dollar bill. His teeth smiled at you evilly in
the store front cases of town dentists. His domed head glinted
suggestively each time you opened the ice box and reached in for
a fresh farm egg. He had fired off his mouth and sent the circus in
panic to a forest beyond town. And passed a law preventing the
employment of children therein when the poles were going up in
the cold dawn light. Quartermain, Quartermain. Tom thought
of him and knew the hatred that Douglas must know for the
buzzard and the vulture and the snake.

"And here's where the ring was and the man in the black silk
hat saying, 'Ladies 'n Gentlemen!'"

He stood at the exact center of the quiet meadow.

"And up there was where the men and ladies in pink cotton
candy clothes swung on trapezes."

Now the night wind whirled in a great merry-go-round about,
stirring the odors, colors, sounds, tossing tin-cans fitfully in gusts
through the grasses that swished like lions walking, and Tom
staring at the sky through which papers flew and soared, dipping,
to fly again. The whole meadow shook and quivered with the

calliope wind and leaves spun in circles, the boy turning his hand out to them with an invisible whip. His eyes fixed the sky. Birds, crying, flew away.

The wind died.

Tom stood for only a minute longer, then his gaze dropped, his hands dropped. He walked across the meadow. He stood at its rim, and the numerous odors were richly ripened and might last, if savored carefully, if he didn't come too often, until next year, until another late spring and summer. Even on winter nights, if you came here, if the wind was right, and the night not too full of moon, anything might happen.

"This is where it was, all right," he said to himself.

And he walked away from the rich meadow, back into the summer night town.

THE CEMETERY
(or THE TOMBYARD)

I T HAD BECOME a familiar pattern by now. Every summer, on a certain July Sunday, they packed themselves into the open air Kissel and thundered out on quiet highways, down dirt roads and through woods to Green Ravine Rest, and here on every hand, as numerous as tenpins, lay relatives, aunts and cousins who had died at night, uncles who had died at high noon, fathers and mothers and sisters and brothers who had wanted to grow up to be firemen and nurses and now were nailed into packets and crossed with stones. And always, starting four years back, Charles had run off, alone, among the horrified stones, frozen at what they represented, and he would fumble his fingers over the chiselled names, reading, with eyes shut, in silent Braille, whispering the name he touched: "B, A, N, G, L, Le, y. Bangley! Died 1924." And on and on, more names, more wanderings. And four years ago he had happened on this one stone building in the ravine, tried the door, found it open, and entered into silence. Oh, how frightened had the aunts been, and the cousins scurrying to find him. But he had waited until he felt like it and come out, not telling where he'd hid. Saying he had simply run off. It meant a licking, but it was worth it.

He would hear them calling, far off in the tomb ravine, among the summer butterflies and the green moss echoes, shouting down the long throat of the underground tunnel, standing by the solemn, reflecting creek, hands up to mouths, calling, calling for him. And he would giggle, stifling his laughter inside, like corking water into a jug. And he would run still further away from them, among the mushroom tombstones that grew up like bits of white cheese and moonstone in the shadows of the summer day. In this land of ravine silence, his feet pattered with the sound of rain along the soft paths of grass, and the further he ran, the more numerous the names on the stones became, Belton, Sears, Roller, Smith, Brown, Davis, Braden, Jones. Lackel, Nixon, Merton, Beddoes, Spaulding. A land of names and silences. And far far away his mother and his father and his aunts and his cousins calling his name:

"Charles, Charles, Charles, Charlie, Charles!"

He stopped when he reached his particular tomb building, slipped wide the door with the broken lock and hurried in. It was a tomb like a wedding cake, fancifully ornate, impossible and lovely. It had four windows facing the directions of the compass, looking out upon moss silence and weeping trees and fluttering water shelves that lowered themselves down a shadowed hill into the tunnel. Along the path now, like a string of white butterflies, flew the girl cousins, hair yellow on the air, eyes flashing.

"Charles, Charles, Charles, Charlie!"

And after them, more serious at the game than the children, came the tall aunts, their white skirts winging on the still air, panic making them begin to stumble and whirl about. "Charles!"

SIXTY SUMMERS burned the grass and sixty autumns plucked the trees to emptiness, and sixty winters froze the creek waters and cracked the toppling stones, while winds raced cold about, and sixty springs opened up new green meadows of color where butterflies were thick as flowers, and flowers as numerous as butterflies.

And then, one autumn afternoon, with the sky iron cold and the wind hurling tins of thunderous and invisible sound through the flying trees, an old woman edged along the path, peering here or there, alone, as delicate as chaff, as yellow as the last leaf.

She paused before the tomb building and nodded and sighed. She went to the long remembered window and peered in. Dust was thickened on the outside, and this she removed with her dainty flowered handkerchief, slowly and tremblingly.

And there was the small boy, leaned against the high sill, in the silent darkness, looking at her, looking out at silence and autumn hardness and the bare earth, and this old woman returned after so long. There was his head, like a dried fruit, and the fragile, time-worn arm and delicate fingers.

"Charles," she said to the window, standing back. "Charlie. I thought of you today. For the first time in years. How long's it been? Sixty years. I forgot all about you. After that first year. I went to Philadelphia and forgot all about it. I thought it was only a dream. And I was married and had children and now my husband's gone and I live alone, and I'm old, seventy years old now, Charles, and I was sitting in my house, for I came back to this only a year ago, and I looked at the sky this morning and suddenly I remembered. It was like a dream, I couldn't believe it, so I had to come to be sure. And now I see it's true, here you are. And I don't know what to say."

The small child looked out through dust and glass.

"I'm sorry, Charlie, do you hear me, I'm sorry. It's too late, but I'm sorry. But listen, Charles, listen. My life is over and it's just as if it never was. When you're seventy it's like an instant. And now I'm here to where you were and have always been, and you shouldn't be jealous and hate me, for it comes to all of us, and now it's coming to me."

SUMMER'S END

SUMMER WAS COMING to its own end, winding up the spool, shaking out the last bright sand from the glass. It took in its leaves, or dropped them when a good wind passed. It let the rain wash the color from the grass. It forgot the flowers so they turned away and died. There was a great stir, as of a family upon the eve of departure, birds rushing all about in children's bands, impatient for the going. When summer died there was always a great whining and roaring of wind. In every yard, soon, summer would be piled and burned, with children tending the pyres and the smoke flagging the sky, showing the birds how the wind moved and where the great waiting south lay.

"The sooner we freeze the sooner we thaw," said Grandfather. "Look at the leaves. The air smells like an old book store on days like this."

The fruits were quartered and liquored and bottled and shelved. The house was painted and shingled and puttied and put right. The trees were free of their leaves and enjoying the freedom of the sky, like hands fresh out of gloves. An avalanche of coal tinned and chuted in a dark pour through the cellar window, rising to a volcano peak in the wooden bin. Winter coming on with stony thunder! Winter, later, floating down like the white lace of a woman passing by. Winter and the flood of wind rising foot by foot over the porches and towers and roofs of town until all was under its tide. The skies swept clean of birds, erased, it almost seemed, by hurrying clouds. Storms coming and going so high that they were not felt, but occurred only among themselves, in high gray mountains in the heavens, throwing lightning and coldness all about in twists and turns. All pointing toward that morning when one would wake to hear the world holding its breath, and silence, in lace, falling from the sky, a whiteness moving in a great moth wind softly upon the lawns. All these things predicted and foretold by this one day in September.